Once Bitten, Twice Shy . . .

Goldie and the wolf hit the ground with a snarl, a
thump, and another shrill, beseeching squeal, the wolf
chomping into Goldie's upper right shoulder. Quickly,
as the two rolled together down the slope and between
two fir trees, Longarm shucked his Winchester from
his saddle boot, racked a cartridge into the chamber,
aimed, and fired.

His bullet ruffled the charcoal fur on the beast's
hindquarters just as it prepared to bury its fangs into the
outlaw's neck, which was protected by nothing more
substantial than a knotted, dirty blue muffler. The wolf
yipped with a jerk, glanced angrily back at Longarm,
yellow eyes glowing in the morning's dullness, then
leaped into the air, twisted around, and dashed off down
the slope through the trees, snarling . . .

➤ TABOR EVANS ◄

LONGARM

AND THE
CRY OF THE WOLF

JOVE BOOKS, NEW YORK

THE BERKLEY PUBLISHING GROUP
Published by the Penguin Group
Penguin Group (USA) Inc.
375 Hudson Street, New York, New York 10014, USA
Penguin Group (Canada), 90 Eglinton Avenue East, Suite 700, Toronto, Ontario M4P 2Y3, Canada
(a division of Pearson Penguin Canada Inc.) • Penguin Books Ltd., 80 Strand, London WC2R 0RL,
England • Penguin Group Ireland, 25 St. Stephen's Green, Dublin 2, Ireland (a division of Penguin
Books Ltd.) • Penguin Group (Australia), 707 Collins Street, Melbourne, Victoria 3008, Australia
(a division of Pearson Australia Group Pty. Ltd.) • Penguin Books India Pvt. Ltd., 11 Community
Centre, Panchsheel Park, New Delhi—110 017, India • Penguin Group (NZ), 67 Apollo Drive,
Rosedale, Auckland 0632, New Zealand (a division of Pearson New Zealand Ltd.) • Penguin Books
(South Africa) (Pty.) Ltd., Rosebank Office Park, 181 Jan Smuts Avenue, Parktown North 2193,
South Africa • Penguin China, B7 Jiaming Center, 27 East Third Ring Road North,
Chaoyang District, Beijing 100020, China

Penguin Books Ltd., Registered Offices: 80 Strand, London WC2R 0RL, England

This is a work of fiction. Names, characters, places, and incidents either are the product of the author's
imagination or are used fictitiously, and any resemblance to actual persons, living or dead, business
establishments, events, or locales is entirely coincidental.

LONGARM AND THE CRY OF THE WOLF

A Jove Book / published by arrangement with the author

PUBLISHING HISTORY
Jove edition / March 2013

Copyright © 2013 by Penguin Group (USA) Inc.
Cover illustration by Milo Sinovcic.

ISBN: 978-0-515-15306-4

JOVE®
Jove Books are published by The Berkley Publishing Group,
a division of Penguin Group (USA) Inc.,
375 Hudson Street, New York, New York 10014.
JOVE® is a registered trademark of Penguin Group (USA) Inc.
The "J" design is a trademark of Penguin Group (USA) Inc.

PRINTED IN THE UNITED STATES OF AMERICA

10 9 8 7 6 5 4 3 2 1

ALWAYS LEARNING   **PEARSON**

*Tabor Evans offers his apologies to real wolves,
who bear little resemblance to
the purely fictional wolves in this story.*

Chapter 1

Katarina Barkova lifted her head from working at her desk near the ticking woodstove. She wrinkled the skin above her fine, long, alabaster nose and cast her frosty, blue-eyed gaze toward an open window at the other end of the little log schoolhouse that sat in the woods near the village of Little Bucharest, in the San Juan Mountains of southern Colorado Territory.

The young schoolteacher had heard something. It had sounded like a dog's growl. Very low. Menacing.

It had seemed to emanate from just beyond the window that Katarina had opened to allow in a little air when she'd inadvertently over-stoked the woodstove. The school day was over, but she'd decided to spend an extra hour at her desk, catching up on her grading before heading back to the village and the house she shared with her parents.

The growl had sounded so menacing, in fact, that

Katarina felt a twinge of uneasiness between her slender shoulders.

She set her pencil down near the composition she'd been grading, slid her chair back, wincing at the grate of the legs against the scarred puncheons, and rose. She stared toward the window, frowning, hearing something else—a soft snorting sound, barely detectable above the slight wind blowing up the canyon along the creek. A ponderosa pine stood just beyond the window, its needles touched with the honey of the late-autumn sunshine.

One of the branches nudged the wall to the left of the open window.

Could that be what she'd heard?

Katarina moved out from behind her desk—a radiant, slender, high-busted blonde of twenty years, in a plain black wool skirt and frilly shirtwaist that drew taut against her full, womanly breasts—and strode to the front of the school along the aisle between the students' simple, wooden desks. A few feet in front of the square, glassless window, she stopped.

It was warm in the school—too warm—but she felt gooseflesh rise along her arms and over her breasts that were trussed up behind her whalebone corset, which unfortunately did nothing to detract her young male students' attention from her ripe bosom.

The low growl came again. It caused Katarina's throat to contract and her mouth to dry.

But then she heard the soft thud of human footsteps beyond the window, and a man appeared in the field of her vision. Herman Walenski, who cut firewood for the school, walked along the trees that lined Crazy Bear Creek. The aspens, cottonwoods, and mountain elms were in full autumn blush, each leaf fairly glowing like its own separate lamp in the afternoon's cool sunshine.

The tall, gaunt man in ragged wool trousers and a wool vest under an even more ragged wool coat, turned his head toward Katarina as he continued walking from her left to her right, along the trees and the stream glittering within them. He wore a black wool watch cap, its leather bill speckled with sawdust, as were the shoulders of his brown coat. His eyes were set deep in dark sockets, mantled by a heavy brow. His cheeks were sunken. He was a sullen, brooding man, but now a rare smile spread his thin lips back from crooked, yellow teeth. It was a customarily odd smile, one that did not reach his dark eyes.

"Afternoon to you, Teacher," he said in his native Romanian.

To which Katarina replied in the same tongue: "Beautiful afternoon, is it not, Mr. Walenski?"

The woodcutter spread his lips wider, gave a cordial nod as he continued walking, holding a long-handled, silver-bladed axe over his right shoulder, and said, "Lovely, indeed."

"Is there a dog out here?"

Walenski looked around, shrugged, and lifted a gloved hand palm up. "I see no dogs, Miss Katarina." He pinched his hat brim. "Good afternoon to you, Teacher."

He disappeared around a bend in the copse of glowing trees, scarlet and yellow leaves dancing in the air behind him. Katarina leaned forward to look out the window in both directions. She stared into the trees near the creek. No sign of the dog. She glanced up at the pine bough scratching the corner of the schoolhouse. It was barely moving now, but that must have been what Katarina had heard.

There was a scraping, groaning sound, and Katarina wheeled, gasping and slapping a hand to her chest with a start. But it was only the back door opening. Anatol Moldova stepped in, smiling shyly, a spray of autumn wildflowers in his large, brown hands, thickened from his work repairing wagons with his father, the mayor of Little Bucharest.

"I am sorry, Katarina!" he said, his blue eyes nearly popping out of his head when he saw how badly he'd startled her.

"Oh, Anatol!" Katarina said, laughing and leaning back against the windowsill. "You did give me a start, but I am very happy to see you!"

Anatol walked toward her—a deliciously handsome young man, two years younger than Katarina, and built strong and square through his shoulders. His face was like a Transylvanian peak scoured and polished by many winds, snows, and blazing suns, his eyes the blue of a springtime lake. His teeth behind his peach-colored lips were hard and white, as strong as the rest of him. His arms were powerful, like the limbs of sturdy oak.

She walked to him, her fears fading like wood smoke on the morning breeze. Just before she reached him, she threw her hands toward him, palms out, halting in mid-stride. She turned to look out the window behind her and out the one to her right, no longer worried about any rabid dog but afraid that one of her students might still be lurking around the school or, worse, that her father might be taking a stroll through the woods to check on her.

Katarina's chastity was her parents' biggest concern,

for they knew what a spell she seemed to cast on all the boys, and even the men, of the village. When she married, she must be as pure as the April rains. What would happen if they and the entire village got wind that their young schoolteacher was cavorting with one of her own students—one a whole two years younger than she was!

Relieved to see no one about, she stifled a chagrined laugh at her naughtiness and walked back to close the front window behind her. When she'd closed the window on the schoolhouse's north side, she fairly ran through the desks to Anatol and let the handsome young man sweep her up in his arms.

She kissed him deeply, sucking at his tongue, letting him suck hers.

"Katarina, the flowers I brought you!" Anatol intoned when, releasing her, he saw that he'd squeezed them in his big, brown fist, tearing many of the stems and blossoms.

"That's all right, Anatol." She stood on her tiptoes to lace her hands behind his neck and press her swollen bosom against her lover's broad chest. "I have another flower for you. I believe it's about to blossom most fully!"

"Katarina!" the boy scolded, shocked and delighted. "It's only four o'clock in the afternoon and the sun is still high. Someone might come along!"

"No one will come, Anatol. And if they do, they won't find us."

In the past, they'd made love in the woods at dusk, when Anatol had been supposed to be out gleaning wood from the forest or hunting for his parents' supper table. At that time, Katarina's family believed her to be working late at school—what a conscientious and hardworking teacher their beautiful daughter had turned out to be!

Now she took her lover's big, brawny, work-calloused hand in her pale, delicate one. "Come, Anatol."

"But where, Katarina? I just saw Walenski strolling through the woods with his axe!"

She smiled up at him foxily, squeezing his hand in hers. "I've found a much better, safer, and quieter place in which to suck your cock, Anatol. Come, quickly!" she hissed, and turned and led him to the schoolhouse's back door.

"Katarina, if we're found out, our fathers will whip each of us bloody! We'll be run out of town and allowed never to return!"

At the door, Katarina turned to him, reached up, and placed two fingers against his warm lips. "Then we'll run away together, Anatol. We'll go to Mexico and live on the Sea of Cortez. Remember how I told you all about the Sea of Cortez—the sands and the salt water? The warm sun will bake right through us. No more long winters trudging through snow as high as our hips!"

"I like it here," he whispered, placing his hands on her shoulders. "I want to stay right here in the woods with you forever, Katarina. I want to marry you someday."

"Shh." Katarina giggled. "Not so serious. We're young. We're meant to have fun before we're tied down and boxed in like our parents." She turned to the door, opened it slowly, and looked out.

There was nothing behind the schoolhouse except the woodshed and the privy, to which a well-worn path led. The path branched to the left, leading to the shed. Nothing moved except the long, tan grass blowing in the breeze. Katarina remembered the low growl she'd heard, and she turned to Anatol standing behind her, his arms around her waist.

"Anatol, did you see anything just before you arrived at the school? I mean, did you hear a dog prowling around?"

He frowned, shook his head. "I heard nothing, Katarina. Come on, now." His broad face broke into a lusty smile. "You've got me all worked up, Katarina. Let's go to this love nest you were talking about!"

Katarina laughed huskily as she took his hand and led him out of the school and down the path, taking the left tine to the woodshed. The building was open on three sides and nearly filled with wood that old Herman Walenski had cut, split, and neatly stacked. There was a narrow aisle leading through the wood at the middle of the shed, and along the aisle Katarina led Anatol.

At the rear of the shed was a gap between the shed wall and the wood that was stacked nearly six-and-a-half feet high. Here, Katarina had arranged wool blankets and a thick quilt on top of a thick pile of straw and wood shavings. There was even a straw pillow covered in striped blue ticking.

"For us?" Anatol asked, chuckling as he stared down at the love nest.

"For us."

"Won't old Walenski see it?"

"Old Walenski has no reason to wander this far back in the shed." Katarina turned to the big boy hulking over her and pressed her hand against his crotch. "Now, Anatol, pull your pants down and give me that big staff of yours. Do you know that when we were going over the times tables this afternoon, I kept thinking about what I wanted to do with it."

Anatol snorted. "Katarina, you are going to go to hell for the way you think!"

"Don't tell me you haven't been dreaming of plundering me with it, Anatol," she said, looking up at him from beneath her thin, blond brows. "Like last time?"

Snickering, Anatol made fast work of unbuttoning his pants and pulling his already-hard member out of the front slit in his longhandle bottoms. It jutted high, bobbing with each beat of his heart, the head swollen and red. Katarina knelt before him, squeezed the rock-hard organ in her slender hands, pumped him gently until he crooned, and then proceeded to lick the underside of it with excruciating slowness.

She tortured young Anatol with her tongue and then her mouth, sucking the head of his cock for a time, nibbling it gently, before sliding it against the back of her throat and down it until she started to gag. When she could feel him rising toward the crest of his desire, and he was panting and groaning and shifting his weight from one foot to the other, she withdrew her mouth from his cock, kissed the swollen tip of it, and looked up at him, licking her lips with desire.

"Are you ready to punish me for being such a bad girl, Anatol?" she teased.

"Katarina, you're going to make me an old man!" he said, dropping to his knees and rolling onto his back, panting as though he'd sprinted a mile uphill.

Katarina stood and began undressing. She did it slowly because she loved the rapt look that always came over Anatol's face when he watched her take her clothes off. When the whalebone corset came off and her breasts sprang free, his lower jaw loosened and he expelled a raspy breath. Her eyes glittered in the sunlight angling over the wood stacked around them.

Naked, Katarina knelt and sat back on her heels. "Your turn," she told him.

Quickly, Anatol stripped his own clothes off. His body was magnificent. It always took Katarina's breath away—his chest so broad and muscular, his belly flat and corded, arms thick and sinewy. His long, thick cock jutted from a nest of curly, honey-blond hair.

Katarina lay back on the blankets atop the straw and spread her legs for him, causing the rose of flesh beneath her belly button to blossom. Anatol dropped to her knees and mounted her. While she reached between his legs for his cock and, gently nibbling his lips, started to direct it toward her snatch, she glanced up over his shoulder to see two red eyes burning down at her from atop the woodpile.

The eyes were set in a crouching wolf's head. A wolf nearly as large as a bear and as black as midnight. Its lips were stretched back from long, curving, white fangs.

Katarina screamed.

Anatol screamed then, as well, and turned to look up over his shoulder at the snarling wolf that, hackles raised, hurled itself toward him.

Chapter 2

The generals's daughter felt all funny inside when the tall, dark man in a snuff-brown Stetson and longhorn mustache walked into the roadside saloon.

They were high in the San Juan Mountains of southern Colorado Territory, and it was winter, so the stranger was clad in a long sheepskin coat, its collar and lapels trimmed with wool. He held a rifle on his right shoulder, and a long, black cheroot stuck straight out of the left corner of his mouth.

The bulky coat did little to hide the fact that the man walking in out of the cold, dark, snowy mountain night was a big, solid, muscular hombre, indeed. The chiseled, rough-planed face beneath the flat-brimmed Stetson was so browned by the sun as to make him appear faintly Indian. His brown eyes set deep in bony sockets bespoke a hard authority and a rugged manliness that caused the nipples of the general's daughter, Catherine Fortescue, to stiffen behind their corset.

His legs were long, slender, and hard as any caval-ryman's. His hands in their black, fur-lined gloves were conspicuously large, as were his feet clad in low-heeled, mule-eared cavalry boots, into which his striped, whip-cord trousers had been stuffed.

Catherine, sitting at a table with her father and her father's several cronies, sank back in her chair and nib-bled her thumbnail, giving a soft chuckle that only she could hear above the low roar of the drinking crowd. Big hands and feet meant only one thing, her lusty aunt Gwen-doline had once informed her. *Dear, you want nothing to do with a man outfitted with small appendages . . .*

Catherine's nether regions continued to prickle and tingle as the man stood in front of the halved-log door, scanning the smoky room through puffs of his own cigar smoke. Others had seen the stranger, as well, and there had been a gradual decrease in the loudness of the conversations as the crowd appraised the impressive-looking newcomer.

As he looked around as though searching for some-one, his penetrating, brown-eyed gaze met Catherine's. They held for a quick second, and she felt her rich lips quirk ever so silently as a thrill rippled through her. She knew with a woman's instincts that the stranger had, however briefly and unconsciously, shared in the same thrill, a primal inner voice informing him that their bodies would respond to each other like bow and fiddle fashioned by the same craftsman.

The stranger glanced to his left and froze, staring at four men playing cards at a table several yards away, all four humbly dressed individuals with long hair and wild-looking, drink-bleary eyes. They held their heads down, as though cowed, one lifting an eye to glance up at the newcomer sheepishly.

The tall, dark stranger strode over, dragged a vacant chair out from the table of the four card players, and hiked his right boot onto it. He rested his rifle—a Winchester '73, Catherine knew—across that knee, sort of half-aimed at the group before him.

Suddenly, the crowd of twenty or so men and two pleasure girls—all taking shelter from the cold night in the Hawk's Bluff Tavern—fell silent as church mice. The stranger poked his hat back off his forehead and said in a menacingly gentle, even drawl around the cheroot in his teeth—"Well, well, Collie and Ulrich—run you down at last. My question is this: Are you gonna come nice and friendly-like or rolled up in your blankets and tied over your saddles?"

The room was so quiet that Catherine could hear the flames in the near woodstove crackling faintly, the stove's iron ticking, as the four seated men stared back at the stranger. Their eyes were hard now, their faces taut with belligerence. Catherine's breath came short, and she felt warm honey pool in the pit of her belly as one of the four said tightly, quietly, "No way we're goin' back to the pen, Longarm. No way in hell."

The man called Longarm smiled around his cigar. "Have it your way, Collie."

Silence followed, so thick you couldn't have driven a wagon pulled by galloping mustangs through it.

The four men stared at Longarm. Longarm stared back at them. Collie jerked up out of his chair, screaming, "Fuck you, you law-bringin' son of a—"

Boom! Boom! Boom-Boom! Boom!

Catherine jumped with each explosion of the rifle that Longarm had snapped to his shoulder so quickly that the motion had been a smoky blur. Mostly, she'd seen his broad, murky shadow dancing around the floor and the table before him. The explosions had sounded like detonated barrels of dynamite, making Catherine's ears ring.

She'd felt their reverberations through the floor beneath her boots and through the chair she was sitting in. They filled her loins with electricity, and by the time the last echo had faded around the room so that the groaning of wounded men could now be heard, she was squeezing her thighs together, squirming in her chair, sweat popping on her forehead.

"Good Lord!" intoned her father, General Alexander Fortescue, retired, heaving himself angrily up from his chair. "What is the meaning of all this cacophony?"

If Longarm had heard the old soldier wearing a long tailored mink coat and a beaver hat and clutching a fat stogie in his beringed right hand, he didn't let on. The lawman merely stared down at the fallen men on the far side of the table from him, and loudly pumped a fresh cartridge into his Winchester's breech. The ejected casing clinked loudly onto the floor and rolled around his boots.

Three of his quarry were down. A fourth sat his chair stiffly, squeezing his eyes closed and extending his arms straight up in the air above his head, palms forward. He had his chin dipped to his spindly chest clad in a billowy green neckerchief over a ragged, calico shirt and silver-trimmed leather vest. He wore a gold spike through his right earlobe.

"Oh, God," the survivor said, his voice quavering.

"Don't shoot me, Longarm. Christ, that was fast. *I don't wanna die!*"

Catherine thought she could smell urine emanating from the man in the room's warm, smoky air, beneath the stench of beer and whiskey and the sickly sweet perfume of the parlor girls. She clenched her fists under the table and stifled a wild laugh. The urine smell was quickly diluted by the rotten-egg odor of powder smoke.

"Stand up, Goldie," Longarm drawled.

The others in the room were muttering among themselves. Several men sitting nearest the lawman and his prey had thrown themselves to the floor when the shooting erupted, and now they were climbing warily to their feet, quietly gathering hats and coins and playing cards from the floor. One kicked a whiskey bottle; it rolled loudly across the floor before coming to rest against a wood box filled with pine.

"Sit down, Father," Catherine said to the general standing beside her. "You're making a fool of yourself."

The old soldier scowled down at his impertinent daughter. He was a big, puffy man with silver-gray hair and a walrus mustache. Catherine arched an admonishing brow at the man, whom she had many years before— even before becoming the heartrendingly beautiful, ivory-skinned, lush-bodied blonde sitting beside him now—wrapped firmly around her little finger.

The general looked a little sheepishly at the other men around the table—his four moneyed hunting companions from Denver, all of whom, Catherine knew, dreamt in vain of making love to his daughter—and then sighed as he sagged slowly back down in his chair, which creaked precariously beneath his considerable weight.

Meanwhile, the lawman aimed his still-smoking Winchester at the hard case he'd called Goldie. "Stand up."

Goldie stood, keeping his hands raised.

"Toss your hoglegs, knives—everything you got— onto the table right here. Do it slow. One move I think might be just a hair too fast, I'm gonna pop a pill through your ticker."

"Ah, shit," Goldie rasped, moving very slowly as he tossed three pistols and two big knives and one smaller one—an Arkansas toothpick, Catherine thought it was called—onto the playing cards before him, among the shot glasses and beer schooners and whiskey bottles.

Everyone in the room watched in hushed silence right along with Catherine as Longarm walked around behind Goldie, cuffed his hands behind his back, then pushed him over to a square-hewn ceiling support post in the middle of the room, only a few feet from Catherine's and the Fortescue hunting party's table. Longarm shoved the outlaw down to his butt and then he got a short length of rope from the burly barman and tied Goldie's ankles together.

"I'm gonna leave him here till I leave in the morning," Longarm told the room. "Anyone turns him loose, I'll gut you like a fish."

Wearily, he turned to the bar, set his Winchester down on top of it, and asked for a whiskey. As he doffed his hat, removed a glove, and swept a hand through his thick, close-cropped, dark brown hair, Catherine saw a quarter-sized hole in the side of the lawman's coat. Beneath the coat's hem, blood dropped, drip by slow drip, onto the tip of his left cavalry boot.

The general and his hunting friends were now conversing among themselves in disapproving tones while casting dark looks at the lawman leaning against the bar and sipping a shot of whiskey. Maryland rye whiskey, to be exact. Catherine's eyes were riveted on the brawny man-beast, and they hadn't miss a thing he'd done or said since he walked into the room.

For his part, Custis P. Long, known far and wide by friend and foe as Longarm, hadn't missed much about the girl, either. In the corner of his left eye, he saw her slide her chair back and rise from her table.

Her father said something too softly for Longarm to hear, and she didn't pay attention to the rotund oldster anyway, as she walked around the table and approached him. Longarm felt the draw of this girl deep in his loins, despite the bullet that had clipped his left side a couple of hours ago, when the escaped prisoners he'd been chasing into the mountains bushwhacked him and left him for dead, though he'd only been feigning it.

He turned to her now, resting an elbow on the edge of the plank-board bar, and let his probing male gaze rake her up and down, just as her eyes had been doing to him since he'd entered the Hawk's Bluff Tavern.

She stopped in front of him, attracting the glances of most of the other males in the place and even the two slightly peeved-looking doxies. Longarm had a feeling this blond, with lustrous hazel eyes and a heart-shaped face right out of an expensive cameo, would attract curious, admiring, longing gazes from both sexes anydamn-where she went.

Her eyes were as cool as shallow water over polished green pebbles as she said just as cooly, "Lawman, eh?"

"Who's askin'?"

Ignoring the question, she glanced at the hole in his coat. "You appear to be lacerated."

"That?" Longarm glanced down at the blood staining his left boot toe. "I've cut myself worse shavin'."

"Nevertheless, blood is blood, and we only have so
much. You need tending, and I'd like to apply for the
job." She lifted one corner of her mouth as her eyes held
steady on his.

"What are your qualifications, Miss, uh . . . ?"

"I have one hell of a bedside manner."

Longarm glanced behind her at the old, mustached
gent in the fringed buckskin tunic under an open mink
coat, who was talking with his pals while looking critically at the beauty standing before Longarm. "What's
Daddy gonna say?"

"How do you know he's my father?"

"If he was your husband, I'd have had to shoot him
by now."

She blinked slowly. "I've trained Daddy well." She
glanced at the low, soot-stained ceiling. "Shall we?"

Longarm glanced at the barman, who was drawing
a beer at the spigot down the bar aways. "Apron, I'll
take a room and a bottle of that rye."

"Ain't got no more rooms," the burly bartender said
in a thick, gravelly voice around the loosely rolled quirley smoldering between his lips. "All taken. Cold damn
night."

"Just the bottle, then," the girl said to the barman,
while staring at Longarm. "I have a room."

Longarm glanced at the old man again, who was
looking toward him and his daughter edgily, squinting
his eyes through billowing cigar smoke.

"Like I said," said the blonde, "I've trained him well."

Longarm paid for his bottle and grabbed his
Winchester.

"Hey, what about them boys you beefed?" asked the barman, nodding his head toward the men bleeding out at the far side of the now-vacant table.

Longarm followed the man's glance and puffed his cigar. "Wolves need feedin', too," he said. "Haul 'em outside. Take what money they got on 'em for payment. My horse is outside—an army bay. Have someone stable him, tend him good, and haul my gear to the girl's room. Just pile it outside the door."

He gave the man a wink and was about to continue forward when one of the men from the general's table stood up before him. He was a youngish, sandy-haired man with a thick mustache and a dimpled chin. He might have been handsome if his copper eyes hadn't been set so deep and close together.

"Just a minute, there, mister . . ."

"Outta the way," Longarm said. "The lady's in a hurry."

The dimple-chinned gent held his ground, lifting a hand and placing its palm against Longarm's chest. "What do you mean by walking in here and causing so much racket? Don't you know the general or his daughter might have been hit by a ricochet? If you're a lawman, you should have taken your would-be prisoners *outside* and arrested them out *there*."

Longarm scowled at the man. He looked at the hand on his chest. There was a gold ring on the pinky. The man grew a little pale around the nubs of his cheeks, glanced at his hand, and slowly, sheepishly lowered it to his side.

Looking at the dimple-chinned gent as though he were a gob of dog shit on the floor before him, Longarm said, "Step aside."

The dimple-chinned gent's eyes blazed, and his jaws hardened. But then, looking up at Longarm's implacable, weather-beaten features, the lawman's head a good three inches higher than his own, he stepped to one side and shrank back down in his chair.

The girl stood waiting, sort of half-smiling, at the bottom of the stairs at the back of the room.

Longarm followed her up. He stared unabashedly at her blue jean–clad ass. Outside of Cynthia Larimer's ass, it was the best ass he'd ever seen.

It was just what the doctor had ordered.

Chapter 3

Longarm followed the girl to a door at the end of the second-story hall. She paused and fished a key out of her gray denim trousers that fit her snugly, revealing the delicious curve of her hips and the tautness of her long, slender legs. "That was my father's assistant, Captain Sidney Ashton-Green," she said in her sexy, husky voice, looking Longarm up and down once more. "I don't believe anyone has ever spoken to him so . . . carelessly . . . since he was in grade school."

"'Bout time then," Longarm said, following the girl into the room.

She closed the door and turned the key in the lock. "Take your coat off. Best take your shirt off, too."

A red lamp burned on the room's dresser. It was a small room. The brass bed occupied most of it, set against the back wall in which a window was shuttered against the night. A charcoal brazier blazed in a corner. The room smelled slightly of cherries and talcum—a feminine smell. Longarm drew a deep draft of it into his lungs. He'd been on the trail of the prisoners who'd escaped from the federal pen in Julesburg for six weeks, and he hadn't seen, much less bedded, a woman in that time.

His loins were heavy with the need. Heavier now as he stared at the rich, honey-blond hair curling down over the collar of the man's wool plaid shirt the girl wore, behind which her breasts jutted, proud and full.

She'd gone to the dresser, and now as she turned up the lamp, she glanced over her shoulder at him. She caught him staring at her, smoke from the cigar billowing around his head. She smiled, blinked slowly, and turned away. "I said take your clothes off, mister."

Longarm grinned around the cigar and leaned his rifle against the wall by the door. "You said take my coat and shirt off."

"Did I?"

She went over to the washstand at the foot of the bed and poured water into the basin. She added a splash of tanglefoot from a labeled bottle—labels on liquor bottles were few and far between this far out in the high and rocky—standing next to the basin and grabbed a cloth off a nail in the wall paneled in vertical, unadorned pine planks. Splashing some of the liquor onto the rag, she turned to face him.

"But why waste time, really?" she said. "We'll be pulling out early in the morning."

Longarm shrugged out of his sheepskin mackinaw, hung it on a spike in the room's closed door. He unbuckled his cartridge belt with its single, cross-draw holster and double-action Frontier Colt .44. He draped the rig over a front bedpost and buckled it. The Colt was never far out of its owner's reach, and it wouldn't be tonight, for he knew that the escaped prisoners had been in these mountains to meet up with members of their old gang.

The girl leaned back against the dresser, holding the bottle in one hand, the rag in the other, watching him with catlike eyes, her rich, red lips parted just enough so that he could see the gleaming, white teeth. The lamp and the charcoal brazier filled the room with dim, umber light and dancing shadows, and it illuminated little gold flecks in her hazel eyes.

Longarm hung his brown tweed frock coat on another bedpost and then kicked out of his boots as he pulled his shirttails out of his pants. He unbuttoned the blue woolen garment and tossed it to the girl. She smiled as she caught it out of the air, and the movement mussed her hair attractively as she coolly threw the shirt onto a near armchair.

A groan sounded from behind the wall flanking her. Longarm froze, frowned.

"What the hell was that?"

"Murphy," the woman said. "Feelin' poorly. We're on the way to the village of Crazy Kate, takin' him to see a sawbones. We heard they had one over there."

Longarm knew the village. He was heading there himself. The town, mostly populated by Romanian immigrants, and which had once been called New Romania, had a town marshal and a jail tight enough to house his prisoner while he scoured the nearby ridges for the other members of Goldie's Gang.

The groan came again, raspy and anguished.

"What happened to him?" Longarm asked as he sat on the bed to peel his whipcord trousers down his legs.

"Wolf bit him," the girl said, as she set the bottle and the cloth on the dresser and began unbuttoning her shirt, behind which her breasts were rising and falling sharply.

"Bad?"

"Bit his leg. Torn it open pretty good, but he should make it." She shrugged out of the shirt to reveal a thin chemise and corset beneath. Her arms were long and the same skin tone as her face—polished ivory.

Longarm felt his longhandles grow tight across the crotch. He flung his pants on the floor and stripped his longhandle top down his arms and then peeled it down his waist. It had shrunk so that it fit his big, hard frame like a second skin. He peeled the bottoms down his legs. His cock bounced free and stood at attention, the head swollen. He heard the girl draw a breath.

Longarm looked at his bloody right side. The bullet had clipped him about three inches above his hip.

"Here," the girl said, and tossed him a towel. "Hold that against it so you don't get blood all over the place."

Longarm pressed the towel to his side while the girl continued undressing slowly before him.

Naked, he leaned back on the bed, propped on his elbows, and watched her remove the chemise. When she'd gotten the corset untied, her breasts fairly leaped from the tight confines, and the corset dropped to the floor at her long, pale feet. She shook her hair back, though some of it remained curling onto the tops of her breasts, and it delightfully jounced across her shoulders.

Her nipples stood up like ripe cherries.

Longarm sighed. His cock grew harder.

Footsteps sounded in the hall. There was the thud of someone dropping something in front of the girl's door.

"That'd be my whiskey," Longarm said.

"You stay there." Catherine walked to the door and opened it without any sign of modesty. She bent forward, giving Longarm a view from behind that made his heart turn a somersault in his chest. She hauled his saddlebags inside, dropped them on a chair, and handed him his bottle of Maryland rye. Then she fetched her own bottle and set both of them on the floor at Longarm's feet.

He watched her full breasts slope downward then jostle as she straightened and fetched the washbowl from the stand. The water steamed.

"I had the houseboy heat some water for my sponge," she said, "just before you arrived."

He popped the cork on the rye and offered her the first sip. She took it then wiped her mouth with the back of her hand and returned the bottle to him.

"Don't let me ruin your bath," he said, and took a long pull of the rye.

"You already have." She splashed more tanglefoot on the cloth. She tossed her head to throw her hair back, glanced casually at his cock, and said, "My, my . . . ," as she sat on the edge of the bed beside him and began dabbing the cloth against the bloody burn in his side.

The whiskey felt like a porcupine raking up against the wound. He sucked a sharp breath and, still leaning on his elbows, threw his head back, as well, stretching his lips away from his teeth. He felt his cock start to dwindle. She saw it as well, and, while holding the burning cloth against the wound, leaned over his right thigh and dropped her mouth down over the head of his staff.

Her warm, silky mouth contrasted the burn in his

side, and he flexed his toes and groaned as a complex tangle of pain and pleasure equaling near-euphoria rippled through him.

She lowered her mouth halfway down his cock, pressing the swollen head against the back of her throat, then lifted her head and smacked her lips as the shaft stood up tall and throbbing once again.

"That's better," she said, and continued scrubbing his wound.

While she worked on the bullet burn with one hand, she fondled his cock very lightly with the other, running just the tips of her fingers up and down his cock and across his balls that sagged down over the edge of the bed.

"You really know how to torture a fella," he rasped.

"Am I hurting you?"

Longarm took another deep swallow of rye. "Real bad."

"Let me know if you'd like me to stop."

He glanced down at her hand manipulating his iron-hard shaft and then at the cloth that had nearly cleaned all the dried blood from around the bullet graze in his side. "You seem like the sorta girl who finishes a job once she starts it."

She smiled, then leaned down once more and took his long, hot, throbbing length into her mouth. She sucked him expertly until he came, spurting his jism down her throat while she held her mouth taut against him. She gagged as she swallowed, her own body quivering, scissoring her long, bare legs against him, her throat expanding and contracting against the head of his shaft and increasing his pleasure until he thought the head on his shoulders would explode, as well.

When he'd spent himself, she lifted her head, tossed her hair back in that deliciously sensual, female way of hers, swallowed, and drew a deep breath. "Christ, I thought I was going to drown!"

She took the bottle from him and took a long pull, not reacting to the harsh burn. Obviously, she was accustomed to hard liquor.

Longarm flopped back against the bed, his muscles still reverberating from the pleasure of her mouth. The preliminaries out of the way, she finished cleaning the wound and then bandaged it while he lay dozing dreamily beside her, taking occasional drinks from the bottle. When the bandage was secure, he rose to a sitting position, placed his hands on her shoulders, and lifted her up onto the bed, so that they were both lying lengthways on top of it.

"Aren't you tired?" she said, smiling and brusquely rubbing her hands through his close-cropped hair. "After being wounded and having, if you don't mind my saying, one hell of a blowjob?"

"No, but if you want to go to sleep, I can find a warm place in the barn."

She gritted her teeth and drew his head down to hers. "Don't you dare not plunder me with that big organ of yours!" she laughed, reaching down between them and wrapping her hand around his cock, groaning with anticipation when she found it fully erect once more.

Longarm slid the organ of topic between her thighs, which she spread wide for him, grunting and groaning and hooking her hands around her ankles to spread her knees even wider. "Oh, gawd!" she rasped, tipping her head back on the pillow and arching her back. "You're gonna cleave me in *two*!"

He hammered against her for about fifteen minutes, mindless of the racket they were kicking up, with the bedsprings singing and the headboard slamming against the wall with each savage thrust, until he fairly exploded inside of her. She groaned through clenched teeth and released her ankles to dig her hands into his ass as they spasmed together, Longarm thrusting against her while she bucked up against him, welcoming his seed.

Fortunately, someone downstairs, in the drinking hall, was playing a raucous fiddle, and that probably covered most of the racket and even the girl's final, shrill love scream.

Longarm remained suspended over her on his outstretched arms and on the tips of his toes until his prick started softening. He pulled out of her and rolled to the side. She rolled against him, curling into a ball, her hair hiding her face.

"Oh, Christ, you plundered me, all right. I've never been assaulted by anything that big. Who the hell are you, anyway?"

Longarm lay on his back, catching his breath. Sweat glistened on his forehead. He extended a big hand to her. "Custis P. Long of the U.S. Marshals Service. You can call me Longarm. All my friends do."

"Hi, Longarm," the girl said. "I'm Catherine."

"Pleased to meet you, Catherine."

"Likewise."

The girl remained in the fetal position beside him, her forehead and knees pressed against his side. Longarm heard the soft squawk of a floorboard and turned to the door. Beneath the door he could see light from the hall lanterns, and a shadow.

"Be right back," he said, patting the girl's naked ass. "Just gonna stoke the stove a little. Gonna be a cold night."

He dropped his feet to the floor, glanced at the shadow under the door again, and then slid his Colt from its holster and rose.

Chapter 4

Longarm hid the Colt behind his back as he walked naked over to the brazier, crossing in front of the door, and then turned back to the door suddenly, wrapped his hand around the knob, raised the Colt, and drew the door open quickly.

He cocked the Colt as he hardened his jaw at the man kneeling before him, the man jerking his head back to stare up, aghast, at Longarm. He was the young fellow with the too closely set eyes from downstairs, who'd made the last effort to save Catherine's honor.

He'd just opened his mouth to say something, when Longarm grabbed his collar, jerked him forward into the room, and kicked him onto his back.

"Sidney!" the girl intoned from the bed, dragging a wad of quilt up and sort of writhing against it to cover herself. "What is the meaning of this?"

Longarm planted a bare knee on Sidney's chest, pinning the man to the floor, and pressed the barrel of the

Colt against his crimson forehead. "I . . ." he said, his close-set eyes nearly crossing as he stared in horror at the cocked gun being held taut between two forked veins in his forehead. "I was . . . I . . . was . . ."

"Peepin' through the keyhole," Longarm said.

"Sidney!"

"What you got to say for youself, Sidney?" Longarm growled. "You got about three seconds before I drill a pill through your worthless skull!"

Catherine came off the bed, holding a blanket in front of her, though it didn't cover much but her breasts and the silky blond hair between her perfectly sculpted thighs. "Longarm, please," she said, chuckling. "The man you have flat on his back on the floor, and against whose head you are pressing your big pistol, is none other than President Johnson's favorite nephew, Sidney Ashton-Green! Do please let him go."

"Yes, do let me go," Sidney Ashton-Green said evenly, as he continued to stare up at the cocked Colt and the iron-hard, dark brown eyes of the angry lawman glaring down at him.

"This little pissant is the President's favorite nephew, eh?" Longarm said, depressing the Colt's hammer. "Well, in that case I won't kill him." He pulled the gun away from Sidney's head and straightened until he was standing tall, though completely naked, over the cowering dandy, still keeping the pistol aimed at Ashton-Green's head. "I'll just shoot an ear off. That's the punishment for staring through keyholes in this neck of the woods. Maybe I'll send the ear back to the President, tell him he'd best keep his favorite nephew closer to home, lest something more important, like his entire *head*, gets mailed to the White House!"

Catherine set her lovely bare feet on the floor and rose from the bed, holding the inadequate covering before her and chuckled down at the man pressing his back flat against the floor. "Yes, an ear might be all right."

"Please," said Ashton-Green, his broad chest rising and falling behind his white cotton shirt and fancily stitched deerskin vest, trimmed with a gold watch chain. "I do apologize. I'd only heard Catherine bellowing so, and I was worried that something terrible was happening to her."

"No, you weren't, Sidney," Catherine said. "You knew we were fucking like a couple of wild horses, and you wanted to watch." She looked at Longarm. "Forgive him, Longarm. He's a fool, but a harmless fool."

"What the hell's he doing with your old man's hunting party?" Longarm asked in a disgusted tone.

"He's father's . . . well, *Captain* Sidney Ashton-Green, of the United States Cavalry . . . is Father's bodyguard."

"Bodyguard?"

Ashton-Green glared up at Longarm now, as though realizing his life was no longer in danger, though his pride had been badly damaged. He pulled his vest down taut against his broad chest and glared up at the brawny, bronze-faced lawman, who stood a couple of inches taller and at least that much broader.

"Yes, bodyguard, you behemoth!" Ashton-Green's eyes flicked to Longarm's dong curving down against his thigh, and then he looked at the girl standing to his left and holding the blanket negligently against her at once coltish and voluptuous body. "And I don't think your father would approve of your cavorting with savages such as this, Catherine. Good Lord, what are you thinking? Look at him!"

"Yes," Catherine said, lowering her eyes. "Look at him." Her eyes blazed angrily when she lifted them again to Ashton-Green. "Shouldn't you be downstairs guarding my father or something?"

"I'll never understand it," the bodyguard said, jerking his vest down again, cheeks flushed haughtily. "A girl of your station cavorting with . . . with the likes of this!"

He flung a hand toward Longarm and then strode quickly out of the room. Longarm glanced at the man's buckskin pants. They looked brand-new, and they sagged on his ass. Longarm slammed the door behind him.

"Sorry about that," Catherine said. "He's in love with me."

Longarm brushed the girl's chin with his thumb and kissed her sleek neck. "I have a feelin' just about every red-blooded man who runs into you falls head over heels."

As he dropped his pistol back into its holster, she wrapped her hand around his shaft. "Or at least head over cock." Rising up on her tiptoes, she tossed the blanket onto the bed and kissed his lips, pressing her full, firm breasts against his chest and then running her nose against his thick longhorn mustache.

"Come," she said, turning away and drawing the bedcovers back. Let's crawl into bed and snuggle till we fall asleep. I'm absolutely exhausted. You nearly fucked me to death!"

As she got into the bed, Longarm walked over and stoked the charcoal brazier, for real this time, adding a shovelful of coal from a box behind it, and then climbed in beside the girl. He took a long pull from the rye bottle then returned it to the stand beside the bed.

"What's a general and his beautiful daughter doin' up here in these mountains in weather like this?" he asked, settling into the bed. "Ain't it warmer back East?"

Yawning, she squirmed against him and rested her cheek on his chest, playing with the curly brown hair sprouting around his heavy, muscular slabs. "Mm-hmmm. But we decided to spend Christmas this year out at Father's ranch near Sapinero. Father bought the spread six years ago, when he retired from President Lincoln's cabinet in Washington, but we've only visited a handful of times. He lets his foreman run the place, with our fifteen to twenty cowpunchers. I love it there, but Father's business interests lie in Washington and Virginia, and he can rarely get away.

"Anyway, he and several of his business cronies and I came out to spend Christmas here and got socked in by the heavy snows in the mountains to the east, forbidding travel. Father and his pals were getting bored . . . and drunk . . . lounging around the ranch lodge all day, when they came up with the lovely idea of riding up here into these beautiful, rugged mountains and seeing who could shoot the largest wolf."

Longarm chuckled at the decadence of the leisure class.

"We heard that the wolves in the San Juans are especially large and wild." The idea of large, wild beasts seemed to appeal to her. Longarm could feel her nipples coming alive against his side, and she slid her hand down his belly to tickle his cock and balls.

Longarm groaned. Despite how tired he was after the long ride through the snow, he felt himself coming alive again, as well. To get her mind off her hand, he said, "The others down there with the general are all rich, eastern mucky-mucks, I take it?"

"Mm-hmmm. Including Murphy, poor man. Murphy owns a couple of clipper ships and hunts foxes with princes over in England." She smiled. "Do you like that?"

Longarm groaned again. She smiled, gazing up at him with those catlike hazel eyes. She kissed his chest and continued with: "Oh, yes. They're very powerful businessmen from back East. Most of them widowed, like Father, though Murphy's wife ran off with the Prince of Wales."

"Murphy's the one the wolf bit?"

"Yes."

"I reckon he found out how savage the beasts are in the San Juans, eh?"

Catherine sighed as though the attack were an especially annoying inconvenience. "The fool was off evacuating his bladder without his rifle. He didn't see the beast perched on a boulder above him. Father saw it just as it jumped, and he fired, scaring the thing away— good Lord, it was so big I thought at first it was a grizzly bear!—or it surely would have torn poor Murphy's head off." She dropped her tone an octave. "Would have served him right. The fool tried to maul me on Christmas Eve when he and the other 'boys' were drunk on chokecherry wine our foreman's Indian wife made. Potent stuff."

"I'll say you're potent stuff," Longarm said, running his left hand down her back and into the warm crack between her butt cheeks. He ran it still lower, until the tips of his fingers felt damp fur.

She looked up at him again, her eyes sparkling. "How's your wound?"

"You did a damn fine job with that wound."

"Care to ravage me again, Longarm? Not to seem wanton, but having found a real man in the world, I feel I've been trifling with boys."

Longarm looked down. Her hand was wrapped around his fully engorged cock once more, pumping. He sighed. She smiled.

He rolled her onto her back, mounted her, and began driving, as she spread her knees high and wide, throwing her hair into a lovely golden cloud across her pillow.

Longarm rose in the predawn darkness, gently slid out from beneath the regally lovely head of Catherine Fortescue, and dressed quietly. When he'd stepped into his boots, he leaned down to plant a tender kiss on the girl's cheek. She groaned and sighed in her sleep, snuggling deeper into her pillow, and then he donned his hat, grabbed his rifle and saddlebags, and stepped into the hall.

Slinging his saddlebags over his shoulder, he continued walking down the hall on the balls of his boots, hearing men snoring behind the closed doors around him. He assumed that the especially raucous snores were issuing from General Alexander Fortescue himself, exhausted from his own trek through the snow.

Catherine probably kept the general's old nerves tied in knots. What father of hers wouldn't be on constant edge with a daughter so full of unbridled, absolutely unabashed passion? Longarm gave an amused snort, entertaining memories of his and her hijinks of the night before, and quietly dropped down the stairs into the main drinking hall, obscured with heavy, dark shadows, only a little milky light washing through the front windows.

He was happy to see that his prisoner was where he'd left him, tied to the ceiling support post. The man's head was down, chin dipped to his chest, and he was contentedly sawing logs. His greasy, dark brown hair hung down from the thinly haired top of his head, dangling around his shoulders, which were clad in a ratty plaid shirt beneath a cowhide vest.

Longarm hauled a three-for-a-nickel cheroot out of his shirt pocket, struck a lucifer to life on his cartridge belt, and lit up. Puffing smoke, he kicked Goldie's left boot, causing the man's spur to grind against the floor. The escaped convict lifted his head with a gasp, blinking.

"Oh, it's you," he said in his gravelly voice.

"Rise an' shine, amigo."

"Where we goin'?"

"To Crazy Kate. I'm gonna lock you up over there with orders to shoot you if anyone tries to spring you while I'm away, huntin' them you're s'posed to meet up with." Longarm had set his gear on a table, and now with his folding Barlow knife, he cut the rope tying Goldie's ankles together.

"You ain't takin' me back to that federal hotbox. Ain't no way. I'd rather die first."

"That can happen." Longarm unlocked the handcuffs, and Goldie pulled his hands out from behind the ceiling support post, wincing at the stiffness in his shoulders.

"God damn," he crooned, rolling his shoulders. "I lost all feelin' in my arms!"

Longarm grabbed his rifle and his saddlebags off the table. "Get up."

Goldie grunted and wheezed as he pushed himself heavily off the floor, taking his time. "I didn't sleep very well. I'm gonna be grumpy today, Longarm."

That last came out as a grunt as Goldie dropped his head and bulled toward Longarm, who'd been expecting the move. He stepped to one side and slammed the butt of his Winchester '73 down hard against the back of Goldie's neck. The man dropped straight to the floor like a fifty-pound sack of cracked corn, making the floorboards leap beneath Longarm's boots, lifting a racket.

Longarm sighed. "Let's try it again, Goldie."

Goldie groaned. Again, he took his time rising. When Longarm finally had him on his feet, he let him fetch his blanket coat and fur hat from the chair he'd left them on the night before, when he'd been playing poker with his now-dead pards. As Longarm was prodding the outlaw toward the front door, he heard a footfall and a wooden creak behind him, and a woman's voice said softly, "Longarm—that you?"

Longarm turned to see Catherine standing in the shadows atop the stairs, holding a thick quilt around her shoulders. Her legs beneath the quilt shone creamy in the gradually intensifying, winter light.

"Yeah, it's me, Catherine. Just on the way out."

"You going to Crazy Kate?"

"Yup."

"Maybe see you there."

Longarm smiled, genuinely enthused by the prospect, though he didn't expect to be in town long. He had to find the men looking to hook up with Goldie and get them all back to Denver, to his boss, Chief Marshal Billy Vail, for formal proceedings, which likely would mean hanging. They'd killed several guards when they'd busted out of the federal pen.

"Might at that," Longarm said, pinching his hat brim to the girl.

"Be careful out there," Catherine said, in her sexily raspy voice. "Wolves on the prowl."

"Of several breeds," Longarm muttered, turning away from the girl reluctantly and shoving Goldie out the winter door and onto the porch.

Chapter 5

"Damn, did you fuck that little fillie?" Goldie asked, widening his seedy eyes with open veneration and not a little envy as he and Longarm stepped onto the porch. "Holy shit, lawman, that's a load o' fine woman there. Maybe, on the way to Kate, you could tell me how it was. Come to think of it, you're lookin' right tired."

Goldie snickered.

Longarm used his rifle butt to prod the outlaw down off the porch and into the roadhouse yard, wincing as pellet-sized snow clawed his cheeks as it fell from an iron-gray sky. Yips and snarls rose from across the stage road that curved along the perimeter of the Hawk's Bluff Tavern, which doubled as a stage relay station. Tall pines and dark crags stood formidably all around the station, and beyond the trail to the southeast, murky shadows of four-legged figures jostled in a tight pack.

"Ah, shit," Goldie said. "You know what that is?"

"I suspect the coyotes are enjoying a breakfast of your friends, Goldie." Longarm gave Goldie a hard shove that sent the man stumbling off toward the barn and corral that hulked on the yard's north side. "Quit dawdlin' or you'll be joinin' 'em."

"You sure that's only coyotes?" Goldie asked as he walked toward the barn, lifting the collar of his blanket coat up high against his jaws. "Some o' them shadows look too big for coyotes. You know, wolves are known to be partic'larly big an' mean in the San Juans. Lots o' food for 'em, folks say, with all the minin' camps." He glanced meaningfully back at Longarm. "I'm talkin' *human food.*"

"Don't worry," Longarm said. "I'll protect you, Goldie."

Goldie told Longarm to fuck himself. Longarm told Goldie to get on inside the barn and saddle his own horse. "I sure as hell am not gonna do it for you. One wrong move, though, and I'm gonna shoot you and put you out of my misery."

Fifteen minutes later, Longarm and Goldie had saddled their horses and were riding them out of the barn, when Longarm cast a quick glance into the forest on the far side of the stage road from where the yips and snarls still rose. He'd started to turn his horse to kick the barn door closed behind him, when he swung his gaze back to the forest.

At least one of the creatures tearing and pulling and burrowing into the cadavers of Collie and Ulrich and the other man, a half-breed named Norman Two Moons, were just as Goldie had noted—larger than your average coyote. One swung his head toward Longarm, as though he'd read the lawman's thoughts, and Longarm saw the two yellow eyes fairly burning there in the night-like darkness of the woods that the growing dawn light had not yet touched. It was hard to tell because of the dense shadows, but the wolf not only looked as large as a small bear, though much more willowy, he also looked black.

"See there!" said Goldie, nodding his head at the beast. "You see that big son of a bitch? That ain't no coyote. Shuck your rifle an' shoot him, Longarm!"

Longarm stared at the wolf staring back at him, the yellow gaze flickering when the animal blinked. Suddenly, the wolf turned its head forward and lowered it to resume ripping and tearing. The growls and angry, competitive snarls grew louder.

"Shoot him, Longarm!" Goldie encouraged, bouncing up and down in his saddle, his wrists cuffed behind his back. "You see the way he was lookin' at us? Like we was next on the menu? *Shoot him!*"

Longarm kicked the door closed, then curveted his horse and jerked on the reins of Goldie's coyote-dun gelding. "He's got plenty to eat right there," he said, pointing his own army bay westward along the trail that hugged the trees and a creek rippling between ice-scalloped banks. "No point in comin' after us." Longarm believed in killing no beast unless he needed the food or he was under attack. Live and let live, was how he saw it, an attitude he'd acquired from having witnessed and partaken in way too much bloodshed.

"He's a devil, that one," Goldie said as they rode, Longarm leading his prisoner's horse up the trail along the forest and the half-frozen creek, tall, rocky crags rising around them. "You know legend tells there's werewolves in these mountains. Came over with the Romanians who settled around Crazy Kate—right where we're headed!"

Goldie cast a haunted glance behind him, his breath

vapor puffing around his head in the cold mountain air. He wore a Stetson tied to his head with a thick, blue muffler. Longarm glanced back at him and grinned, puffing his three-for-a-nickel cheroot. "Don't worry, Goldie—I'll protect you."

Goldie glared at him, bunching his unshaven, pugnacious face, his dark eyes set deep beneath thin, dark brows. "Fuck you, Longarm. My old man trapped in these mountains back before the war, and he said he seen 'em. Even lost a partner to one. He himself had to shoot said partner when, during a full moon, he turned into a man-wolf. A fucking *werewolf*!"

Goldie threw his head back and howled. It was such an authentic-sounding howl, echoing off the jagged-topped, towering crags, that Longarm felt the skin beneath his shirt collar tighten. When the howl had finished echoing around the deep canyon they were riding through, Goldie laughed.

"Ah, hell, I don't believe that shit any more than you do. But you've heard the legend, haven't you, Longarm?"

Longarm had ridden through this part of the San Juans a couple of times before, and it was hard to pass through even once without at least hearing that there *was* a legend—having to do with a young woman from Little Bucharest, the mining and hide-hunting camp now known as Crazy Kate on account of the legend itself, but he'd never heard the particulars.

He supposed he was going to hear them now. Goldie was one gassy cuss. Likely facing a hangman's rope made him nervous and extra chatty.

Longarm knew he didn't have to respond to the question, so he merely relit his cheroot that the falling snow had put out, and half-listened in a bored sort of way as they rode and Goldie said, "Yessir, I reckon them folks from Romania brought the curse of the werewolves with 'em. An old curse, to hear to tell it. Started way back with Attila the Hun—can you believe that, Longarm?"

Half-listening, Longarm sucked the rich smoke deep into his lungs, and when he had his cheroot drawing again to his liking, he flicked the match into the snow along the trail. It snuffed out with a slight *phfft* that the lawman could hear in the dense silence.

They were climbing a gradually steepening grade toward a pass, so he had to hold the horses to a leisurely pace. Besides, while the stage road had been graded a few days ago, there were a good ten inches of fresh down on it, and that could mean unseen ice patches beneath. The last thing he needed out here was a horse with a thrown shoe or, worse, a broken leg.

"Anyways," Goldie continued, his voice obnoxiously loud in the silence, "a group of Romanians came here to the San Juans and built 'em their own special town, and took up minin' and hide huntin', an such. Queer mountain folks who didn't much like livin' amongst others 'cause they were so accustomed to keepin' their own company back in Eastern Europe, they say. Anyways, as soon as they came, these mountains started attracting wolves. More than usual. And folks started gettin' attacked, eaten. I ain't shittin'—more than a few folks became wolf bait. That caused more than a few of the non-Romanians in the area to light a shuck." Goldie chuckled. "I reckon I can understand lightin' a shuck under such circumstances as those. Anyways, like I was sayin', wolves kinda got a stranglehold on the place, but the Romanians just sorta learned to put up with it. But then somethin' really terrible happened."

Goldie had slowed his voice down, spreading the words out for dramatic effect. Now, peevishly, he called behind Longarm, "Hey, you listenin', Lawman? You really oughta listen to this. Give you more of an appreciation and healthy respect for these wolves, one of which you coulda shot and did not, I might add. That very easily coulda been a fuckin' werewolf!"

"Don't piss down your leg, Goldie. That wasn't no werewolf."

"*Any-ways*," Goldie continued with an air of acutely strained patience, "there was this purty, young schoolteacher named Katarina Barkova. She was spreadin' her legs for one of her boy students out in the woodshed behind the school one sunny autumn afternoon, when— what do ya know—a wolf attacks the boy. Tears him apart bad an' bloody right there in front of the girl. Tears his arms and legs off. Chews out his heart and his liver. The girl herself? Well, she goes mad from the horror of what she sees. Her family locks her up with the nuns in the convent in the mountains overlooking the town, and after they done that, locked her up in there with them nuns, know what she did?"

Goldie stared at Longarm as though actually awaiting a response. Longarm just stared back at him.

"They said she started howlin' with every full moon," Goldie said.

"Of course, she became a werewolf, too," Longarm said, finding himself sort of half-enjoying the entertainment, since he had nothing else to think about and they still had a two-hour ride over the pass to Crazy Kate. These local legends were colorful, if nothing else.

"I didn't make up one word of that, Lawman," Goldie intoned with haughty defensiveness. "Just wanna make that clear. That story there is told an' retold in these here mountains, and they say that to this day, that Crazy Katarina—or Kate, as the locals call her now, there bein' a fairly big mix of folks in Little Bucharest these days—howls like a damn she-wolf in season, puttin' the whole town on edge."

"Suppose she was bit?"

"Musta been. You figure it out." Goldie jerked in his saddle, looking first to one side of the trail and then to the other. "You hear that?"

"Hear what?" Longarm said, glancing over his shoulder.

Goldie looked worried as he scanned the slope rising on their right side, his dark, deep-set eyes probing every nook and hollow of the boulder-strewn, forested mountainside.

"Sounded like something prowling around in the woods"—Goldie turned to stare into the trees on the downslope, toward the creek that was rushing more loudly here, where it was dropping faster—"all around us."

"You're just hearing the stream."

"Fuck the stream. That ain't what I'm hearin'."

Longarm drew his bay to a stop and pricked his ears to listen, raking the area around him with his gaze.

"I sure don't like sittin' this saddle with my hands cuffed behind my back, lawdog. I'm defenseless here. Hell, I couldn't run if I had to!"

"You should have thought of that before you robbed that harness shop in Cisco, and raped the harness maker's wife. And then killed those guards when you escaped the pen."

Goldie cursed the lawman as he looked around warily.

"Well, I don't hear or see nothin'," Longarm said. "Let's get a move on. I'm hungry."

He turned forward and touched heels to the bay's flanks.

"Ah, shit, so's he!" Goldie squealed.

"So's who?" Longarm had barely gotten the question out before a loud snarl rose and he turned around just in time to see a large, charcoal-black creature leap off a boulder on the upslope and swoop Goldie from his saddle with a shrill scream.

Chapter 6

Goldie and the wolf hit the ground with a snarl, a thump, and another shrill, beseeching squeal, the wolf chomping into Goldie's upper right shoulder. Quickly, as the two rolled together down the slope and between two fir trees, Longarm shucked his Winchester from his saddle boot, racked a cartridge into the chamber, aimed, and fired.

His bullet ruffled the charcoal fur on the beast's hindquarters just as it prepared to bury its fangs into the outlaw's neck that was protected by nothing more substantial than a knotted, dirty, blue muffler. The wolf yipped with a jerk, glanced angrily back at Longarm, yellow eyes glowing in the morning's dullness, then leaped into the air, twisted around, and dashed off down the slope through the trees, snarling.

Longarm's Winchester leaped and roared twice more, but his slugs merely chewed bark from pine boles.

Goldie groaned and grunted as he writhed in the snowy brush between the two firs, hands cuffed behind his back. Longarm swung down from the leather and walked over to the man, dropping to a knee.

"Goldie, you poor bastard. How bad he get you?"

The outlaw rolled onto his back with an especially loud grunt, writhing in pain and fear, his face twisted, lips stretched back from his tobacco-grimed teeth. "What'd I tell you, damn your lawdoggin' hide? See what happened? *See?* Why in the hell didn't you listen to me, lawman? Now look what he done! Damn near tore my arm off!"

Longarm glanced toward where the wolf had hightailed it, then set his rifle against a fir. He leaned down over Goldie once more, inspecting the tear in the shoulder of his blanket coat through which blood oozed. "Ah, hell, he didn't get you that bad. Quit carryin' on; you're embarrassin' yourself. What kind of a hard case are you, anyways—can't take a little nip from a puppy dog?"

"*Puppy dog?*" Goldie squirmed from side to side as he hoisted himself to a sitting position with his hands cuffed behind him. He jutted his enraged red face at the lawman, his gold ear spike glinting dully in the gray light. "That wasn't no goddamn puppy dog, you idjit. That was a wolf. Possibly a fuckin' werewolf. And you know what that means?"

"Yeah, I know—you'll be howlin' along with Crazy Kate at the full moon." Longarm stood and looked around. He'd better find a place to build a fire and get the outlaw's shoulder cleaned out and the blood stopped. The killer and rapist didn't deserve it, but Longarm would have some explaining to do to Billy Vail if he let him die from a wolf bite before Billy and a federal judge could get his neck stretched.

"No!" Goldie intoned, his shrill voice echoing. "We can't stay here. They might be all around us. A whole pack of 'em! And, if I remember right, tonight the moon'll be full!"

Longarm looked around carefully. He didn't see anything moving among the trees and rocks—only a few chickadees and nuthatches performing acrobatic feats among the branches as they pecked for grub. His not hearing anything didn't mean much, the lawman realized.

He hadn't heard the wolf that had swooped Goldie out of his saddle. Apprehension and befuddlement weighed heavy on him. He didn't believe any of that gothic shit about werewolves, but these woods were obviously home to a ferocious pack of *real* wolves, just as he'd heard they were. It was strange for a single wolf to attack a man in the daylight, but maybe the beast was especially hungry and had seen that Goldie was defenseless, having his hands cuffed behind him.

"Demons is what these wolves around here are," Goldie said in a low growl, as though offering an alternative explanation, looking around and gritting his teeth. He was still breathing hard, still terrified from the attack.

"Hogwash."

"You could at least uncuff me, goddamnit!"

Longarm walked over and freed the outlaw's wrists from the cuffs. As afraid as Goldie was of the wolves, he wasn't going to try anything against Longarm, who slipped the key back into his coat pocket and walked off down the slope. When he'd found a good place to set up a camp for a short time, he retrieved his horses and gathered wood. Goldie gathered a few sticks halfheartedly, favoring his right side and continuing to look around as though another attack were imminent.

When Longarm had gotten a fire going and had set a pot of coffee to boil with water he'd fetched from the creek, he told Goldie to take his coat off. "I'll see to that wound. Wouldn't want you to die on me, an' cheat the hangman."

"That's real nice of you," Goldie said, unbuttoning his coat. "I'm so mighty pleased to hear your sympathy, lawdog. Fuckin' bastard."

"Goldie," Longarm said, helping the man pull his coat off his right arm, exposing the bloody wound at the top of the arm. He was trying to settle him down, as the outlaw's fried nerves were beginning to singe his own. "Where'd you ever get a name like Goldie? Your hair's brown."

"Goldspoon," Goldie said. "Last name's Gold-spoon."

"Oh, that's right—I remember now." Longarm used his pocketknife to cut the man's bloody shirt around the wound that kept pushing up liver-colored gobs of blood, which dripped over Goldie's shoulder and down his chest, staining his wool shirt and his vest. "From the warrant the prison sent out. Marion Goldspoon."

"I don't go by Marion, so I'll thank you not use that handle." Goldie slanted a look up the wooded mountain on the far side of the creek that ran darkly between snowy, icy banks. "It's Goldie, plain an' simple. How bad's it look?"

"Shit, you've cut yourself worse shavin'." It was a lie. The puncture wounds were deep and widely spaced, the top teeth having laid open the back of the man's shoulder worse than the bottom ones had dug into the top of it. No point in telling Goldie that. Longarm was tired of the outlaw's mewling. "I'm just gonna cauterize it, an' you'll be good to go."

"Ah, shit—you're just gonna love that, ain't ya? Let me get all chewed up, and then burn me with a knife."

Longarm chuckled. He cut it off when a wolf's howl sounded from a ridge up the mountain to the north, on the far side of the trail.

Goldie stiffened. "Shit!"

Longarm scrutinized a jagged crag towering far above the tree line. The black rocks were dusted with snow, the very top of the crag fuzzed with low clouds from which snow continued to fall—large, woolly flakes falling slow. Again, the wolf howled, shrill and echoing, half-mournful, half-menacing.

"Give me my gun, Longarm."

"No."

"What happens if they come? Turns out you ain't as good at protectin' your unarmed prisoner as you claimed to be!"

"You got me there, Goldie," Longarm said, reaching into his saddlebags and withdrawing a small burlap bag. He tossed the bag to Goldie. "You'll find a coupla roast beef sandwiches in there. Help yourself. A saloon girl made 'em for me back in Crestone yesterday."

Goldie raked his gaze from the towering crag that was now suddenly completely lost in the clouds, and then looked into the bag. He withdrew a small waxed paper bundle and unwrapped the sandwich. "Frozen," he said in disgust.

"Might break a tooth, but it'll fill your belly." Longarm had tossed a handful of coffee into the boiling pot and was heating the blade of his Barlow knife in the leaping flames. The blade had turned black and was beginning to glow when the coffee frothed around the pot's rim, the tan bubbles dribbling down the sides.

He set the pot on a rock away from the flames and then went over and knelt down beside Goldie, who slowly tore bits of the sandwich off with his teeth, chewing as though the cold bread and meat hurt his choppers.

He looked at the smoking blade in Longarm's gloved hand. "Ah, shit, this ain't my day. Wasn't my night, neither. I was winnin' big till you showed up and shot the hell out of the boys I was playin' with."

"Bite into that sandwich hard," Longarm said. "This is gonna hurt like hell."

Goldie cursed again then leaned back against the log behind him, braced himself, and stuck one half of the sandwich in his mouth. "Okay," he said around the food.

Longarm pressed the blade against the front part of the wound. The skin melted like wax, and white smoke curled up from the blade, smelling like something dead. Goldie jerked and grunted, grinding his spurs into the ground. Quickly, Longarm removed the blade from the front part of the wound then laid it over the half that angled down over his shoulder, making sure the cauterizing encompassed each of the bloody puncture marks.

Goldie bit the sandwich in two, and half of it dropped to his lap as he threw his head back and groaned, continuing to rake the ground with his spurs.

Longarm lifted the blade, wrinkling his nostrils at the stench of scorched skin and blood, then reached into his saddlebags for a bottle. He popped the bottle's cork, took a pull of the rye, then splashed a little over each cauterized area of the outlaw's shoulder.

It was a sad waste of good whiskey, but it was all he had. By the time the smoke stopped rising from Goldie's shoulder, the outlaw had passed out, sagging back against the log with a ragged half of sandwich clamped in his jaws.

"Ah," Longarm said, "quiet at last."

He took another pull from the bottle then hammered the cork back in with the heel of his hand. Setting the bottle aside, the lawman cleaned the Barlow's blade off in the flames, wiped it with a handkerchief, and returned it to his pocket. He then took the other sandwich out of the burlap pouch, poured himself a cup of black, piping hot coffee, and sat back against a rock on the far side of the fire from the unconscious Goldie.

He looked around as he ate and washed the sandwich down with the coffee. There was no movement except for the dark water of the stream sliding between its banks, and the lazily falling snow, flakes of which sizzled softly on the hot rocks around the fire. The only sounds aside from the cracking flames were the occasional bits of ice cracking off the fingers protruding into the stream, or the soft thud of a branch getting pinned up against the bank.

The silence was dense, almost funereal. He glanced again toward the crag that had been decapitated by a low, heavy ceiling of goose down. Had the wolf really been standing up there?

Was there any possibility that they could be more than just . . . well . . . *wolves*?

Longarm pondered that for about five seconds and then, catching himself, gave a caustic snort. "Christ, I'm gettin' as cork-headed as Goldie."

They might be rabid, but they sure as hell weren't

haunted, though now that he thought about it, he wasn't sure which would be worse.

He finished his sandwich and washed down the final bite with the last of the coffee. He was about to toss the grounds into the fire, when he stayed the movement, lifting his head and frowning, staring downstream. The skin on his lower back began tingling as the faint yipping of a half dozen or so coyotes—or wolves—reached his ears. The gradually loudening cacophony echoed around the canyon, so that it was hard to tell exactly where it was coming from. It seemed to be coming from everywhere down canyon.

The source of the commotion seemed to be gradually growing nearer.

Beneath the yips and occasional howls, hooves thudded. The thudding, too, grew in volume and then it was coupled with men's harried voices. Longarm looked up the slope to see riders coming along the trail, showing glimpses of themselves between the trees. They were jouncing in their saddles, leaning forward, their horses' heads bobbing as they galloped up the slope toward Longarm's position. The riders were all clad in furs— good quality furs, it appeared from Longarm's vantage point.

The general's hunting party?

The yipping continued getting louder in small increments, but judging by how the riders galloping up the trail kept casting wary looks behind them, toward the coyotes—or wolves—they believed the madly yipping creatures were chasing them.

Longarm rose and grabbed his rifle. He looked at Goldie, who must have heard the noise in his sleep. As the outlaw leaned to one side, head sagging toward the ground, he muttered and blinked and moved his lips like a dreaming dog. A dog dreaming about being chased.

Longarm walked over and kicked the man's left boot. "Goldie, get up." He heard the tautness in his own voice. The apprehension. If the yips were coming from wolves, there must have been at least a small pack of the creatures. And from what he'd seen of them so far, he and Goldie had best get on up the trail toward Crazy Kate.

"Goldie," he said, louder, above the thundering of riders' hooves on the trail above him. He turned to see the shaggy line of them galloping on upstream and upslope beyond him, none looking toward him, their attention riveted on the trail ahead or the trail behind.

Longarm's and Goldie's horses snorted and stomped and tugged at their reins tied to pine branches.

Longarm grabbed Goldie's coat collar and pulled the man to his feet and held him there. Goldie stumbled around as though drunk. "Wha—what is it?"

"We're pullin' foot, so get your damn land legs, and get 'em fast!"

Longarm emptied his coffeepot on the steaming flames, kicked dirt, snow, and rocks on the fire, and stowed the pot in his saddlebags. As Goldie looked around, blinking and wincing against the pain of the wolf bite, Longarm brushed past him as he headed for their horses. He slung his saddlebags over the bay's back, behind the saddle, and then slid his rifle into its scabbard.

Meanwhile, the yips and howls and occasional snarls continued to grow louder, but the wolves seemed to be hanging back for some reason. If they were giving chase, it was a slow, cautious chase. Why? Were they aware in the wolfish, cunning brains that their prey had weapons that could hurt them?

Goldie had stopped near the horses and was staring down canyon through the snowy brush and over-arching pine boughs. "Shit, that's wolves, ain't it? They're comin' fer us!"

"I don't know who they're comin' for exactly, but I do know that it sounds like a few of 'em. We'd best haul our asses on up the trail." Longarm went over and grabbed the man's collar, giving him a hard jerk and throwing him against his horse. "Get mounted!"

He didn't bother with the handcuffs. Goldie wasn't going anywhere but where Longarm was heading—to the sanctuary of Crazy Kate.

Longarm swung onto the bay's back and reined the mount up the hill through the pines. The yips and squeals were getting louder, but as he stared down the trail, the fresh snow on which had been ruffled by the passing riders, he saw nothing. There were only trees and rocks and the creek all swaddled in the grayness of the low sky and the lazily falling snow. It was almost as though the wolves, if that's what was out there, were invisible.

Longarm half-scoffed at the thought, but the apprehension dragging cold fingers up and down his back was hard to deny. And he had no explanation for the especially brave, savage wolves he'd encountered in this canyon. Not to mention the disembodied cries he was hearing now.

"Where are they?" Goldie asked, slumped in his saddle, looking miserable, as he booted his dun onto the trail.

"Your guess is as good as mine." Longarm slid his Winchester from the saddle boot, cocked it one handed while he held the reins taut with his other hand, then set the rifle across his saddlebow. He depressed the hammer but kept his thumb on it. "Let's ride."

"Yeah, that's been my point all along!"

Goldie touched spurs to his dun's flanks and trotted the mount off Longarm's left flank, grunting against the pain of his jouncing perch. He kept looking back over his bloody shoulder as he and the lawman followed the scuffed tracks of the hunting party.

"How come they don't show themselves?" he asked. "They sound so damn close. But I don't see 'em!"

"Shut up and ride!" Longarm said, feeling a little foolish as well as incredulous.

He glanced behind, as the yips seemed to be originating from only twenty, thirty yards away, but there was not a single yipper in sight. That couldn't be. It defied logic. His lack of an explanation for the odd events offended his sense of rationality, a trait he'd always prided himself on.

What the hell was going on here?

When they crested the pass, they checked their horses down between towering walls of boulder-strewn cliffs, the cliffs' peaks lost in the clouds. Longarm looked back down the trail threading the bottom of the canyon. It wound away until it looked little more than a white thread between the gray boulders and dark green, black-trunked pines.

Suddenly, the yipping, which had not grown any louder since they'd left the spot where they'd entered the trail, fell silent. There was no tapering off, just a sudden and total silence. It was so quiet in the wake of the shrill yipping that Longarm could hear the soft *snick*ing sounds of the flakes landing on the snowy ground around him.

The horses stared down trail, as well, ears twitching as though they, too, were wondering what had become of the wolves. The lungs of the bay expanded and contracted testily beneath Longarm.

"Shit," said Goldie softly, breathing as hard as Longarm's horse. "What you suppose they're up to?"

"Don't look a gift horse in the mouth, Goldie." Longarm reined the bay around and started down the other side of the pass, the next canyon shallower than the previous one. "Come on."

Longarm glanced back at Goldie. The outlaw sat staring into the pass they'd just left. "Don't make me throw the cuffs on you, Goldie. Come on."

The outlaw shook his head and turned the dun around to follow Longarm down the pass. He rode up to Longarm's left, the snow clinging to his long, greasy, dark brown hair like lice. He looked troubled as he rode along, saying nothing until: "You think I'm one o' them, now?"

"One of what?"

Goldie looked at Longarm sharply. "What do you mean—*what?* A fuckin' *werewolf*!"

"I guess we'll find out later tonight," Longarm said, slanting a glance at the cloudy sky and continuing to ride.

Chapter 7

An hour later, Longarm and Goldie topped the next pass and stared off into another, broader canyon to the west. The clouds had parted and the sun shone through the gaps, but the snow was still falling. It looked like gold dust in the sunshine.

The creek angled away to Longarm's left, running along the base of a high, gray cliff wall devoid of trees. The ground sloped up to the right of the trail, and on a broad shelf, hunkered at the base of the opposite cliff, sat Crazy Kate. It was a shabby collection of dun shacks that were almost indistinguishable from the boulders and thick clumps of brown brush they sat among. If you didn't know a town lay there, you'd have to look carefully before you spotted Crazy Kate.

Up canyon to the west lay the green of more forest behind the hazy white curtain of falling snow. The smell of wood fires touched Longarm's nostrils, bespeaking food and warmth and sanctuary from whatever in Christ's name lay behind them.

Goldie was the first to start down the slope, riding slumped even lower in his saddle. He was eager for a cot even if that cot lay in a six- by ten-foot cell.

Longarm followed him down the gentle grade. At the bottom, the trail forked, with the main tine leading off up canyon and into forested low country, while the right tine angled up the slope through piñon and sage until it became the main street of the village once known as Little Bucharest.

Fifteen minutes later, the shacks and pens and corrals began sliding up around them. Smoke wafted from the stone or brick chimneys of the cabins, most of which sported neat little front porches that were more brightly painted than the usual run of frontier porch. Shutters were painted bright red or spruce green, in the eastern European manner, Longarm assumed. Gardens, brittle and brown with winter, lay in neat rows, some partitioned off from livestock by low stone walls.

As Longarm's bay continued walking into the town, the lawman turned to the north to see the ancient convent sitting precariously atop a flat-topped pinnacle of molded, crenelated rock. The convent was built of native stone, and it resembled the medieval castles that Longarm had seen in pictures of the mountainous, picturesque country the folks who'd originally settled here hailed from—a country that no doubt looked very much like this neck of the San Juan Mountains of southern Colorado.

Longarm looked away and then looked back, for just then he realized he could hear the distant, melodic strains of a hymn drifting down from that high, stony perch. The music was so faint that it was nearly lost beneath the clomps of the horses' shod hooves on the snowy street, but it lent an ethereal, mystical air to a snowy village that could have leaped out of a children's storybook.

Longarm and Goldie entered the main business district, which was about a block long, with several large, false-fronted frame shops as well as adobe brick and log ones. Here the village more resembled a customary frontier settlement, though a saloon on the street's left side boasted a sign above its porch announcing THE CARPATHIAN MOUNTAIN HOTEL AND SALOON. The shutters on its second and third floors were painted bright red, and they fairly glowed in sharp contrast to the dingy copper color of the building's adobe bricks. Elk and deer horns adorned the porch posts.

Longarm knew there were no Carpathian Mountains anywhere around here, so the name must have been a nod to a range back in the Old World. From inside came the strains of a fiddle drowning out the hymn emanating from the stony pinnacle above the village. A half dozen or so horses stood hang-headed in front of the saloon, and a young man in a leather immigrant cap was holding the reins while a fur- and buckskin-clad gent on the porch spoke to him, gesturing toward the horses, as though issuing instructions for their keep. Longarm scrutinized the gent on the porch and shaped a rueful smile.

Sidney Ashton-Green.

As Longarm had suspected, it had been the general's hunting party who'd galloped up the hill past Longarm and Goldie. They were all likely enjoying hot toddies inside the Carpathian, warming their regal, moneyed selves swaddled in fancy buckskins in front of a crackling fire. Including Catherine Fortescue, Longarm speculated, with an involuntary throb in his loins.

He'd head that way soon, but first things first.

The stone jailhouse sat kitty-corner from the saloon, on the street's right side. As Longarm headed toward it, he saw a stocky gent in a brown wool coat standing outside, under the brush roof, leaning forward against the porch rail, a quirley smoldering between his lips.

"Well, I'll be a monkey's uncle—Custis P. Long," said the man whom Longarm recognized as the town marshal of Crazy Kate. The marshal narrowed his eyes with incredulity. "What brings you to this blister on the donkey's ass?" He slanted an eye at the snowy, dull gray sky. "This late in the year . . ."

He had a better memory for names than Longarm did. The federal lawman couldn't remember the local man's handle, just his face. This man had been the lawman when Longarm last pulled through here, three or four years ago. That was a long time for a man to be marshal of the same town. Most either moved on, retired, or were planted in the local boneyard.

This man was blue-eyed, with severely sculpted cheeks the color and texture of raw burger, above a silver dragoon-style mustache. He wore a scarf under his hat, protecting his ears from the cold. He squinted his frosty blue eyes against the smoke drifting up from the cigarette.

"Trouble," Longarm said. "In the person of this man I have here—one Marion Goldspoon, more commonly known as 'Goldie.' Escaped from the federal pen near Julesburg. I ran him and his cohorts down in Hawk's Bluff Tavern. Goldie here's the only one who survived the ordeal."

"Ah, shit," said the town marshal. "And I suppose

you want me to put him up. Feed him. Make him coffee. Empty his piss pot for him."

"And keep his friends from breaking him out, if it comes to that." Longarm swung his right boot over his saddle horn, kicked free of his left stirrup, and dropped straight down to the frozen street. "Don't get your neck up—I'll give you a hand. And my office will compensate you for your time an' trouble, Marshal . . . uh . . . ?"

"He take a bullet?" asked the local badge toter, ignoring Longarm's question and scrutinizing the outlaw now slumped low in his saddle, blood staining his coat.

"Wolf bit him."

The local lawman shifted his severe-eyed gaze to Longarm and then glanced toward the Carpathian Saloon on the other side of the street, from which the kid in the immigrant hat was now leading the general's horses away, likely toward a livery and feed barn. "Folks who rode in ahead of you had the same trouble. Only they lost the man they was bringin' in. A rowdy pack got him, they said. Ripped him right off the travois they was usin' to haul him here. Wanted to know if we had this sorta trouble often around here." He smiled a little devilishly at that.

Longarm winced as he glanced at the saloon. "I'll be damned." No wonder they'd been riding so fast up that slope, risking life and limb. Maybe the fact that the wolves had been fed explained why they weren't in such a big hurry to chase down the general's party, as well as Longarm and Goldie.

Longarm turned back to the red-faced, gray-mustached lawman. "What'd you tell 'em?"

"About what?"

"What do you mean—'about what'? About that sorta trouble," Longarm said, growing miffed at the man's arrogant, snide demeanor.

"I said it happens around every full moon." The man smiled again, the same way as before, and then looked at Goldie, who looked as though he were about to tumble out of his saddle. "There'll be a full moon tonight, in fact. That means your wolf-bit prisoner will have to go in the hole."

"What hole?"

"You'll see."

Goldie looked at Longarm, who'd walked over to the dun to help the prisoner out of his saddle. "What's he sayin' about a hole, Longarm?"

"He's sayin' you're goin' in one."

"You want me to do it or shall I take him down there myself. Or maybe we oughta just shoot him right here and be done with it," suggested the lawman, who seemed to be enjoying himself. "Why waste food and manpower on 'im?"

"Can't argue with your logic, but since I'm a lawman and not a hangman, I reckon we'll have to feed him till I leave here, which I hope is soon." Longarm helped Goldie out of the saddle. When the man stood slumped before him, sort of leaning against the dun, the federal lawman added, "Don't like the idea of gettin' caught up here for the winter."

"One good snowstorm is all it'd take to seal the passes," the local lawman warned.

"Any strangers in town?"

"I ain't seen none but the folks who rode in a half hour ago—the mucky-mucks over yonder. Said they was part of some general's party. Don't recollect the name. Just that one was a right well put together young lady." The local badge toter grinned, showing large, yellow teeth beneath his mustache.

Longarm gave Goldie a shove toward the porch steps. "Let's go, Goldie. You know the drill. Any fast moves and I blow out your spine."

"I wanna know what hole I'm bein' dropped into," Goldie complained as he walked heavily up the porch steps.

The lawman opened the door and stepped back, grinning his malicious grin around the quirley in his teeth. "Come on, son. I'll show you."

Holding his rifle on Goldie, Longarm followed the outlaw into the dingy, smoky office. As the local lawman stepped in behind him, a man sitting at a desk against the front wall dropped his clodhopper boots to the floor with a *boom!* A big man to go with his boots, he jerked a shotgun up with a start, eyes blazing in deep, fur-mantled sockets.

"Emil!" The local lawman admonished the man, his deep voice echoing off the office's rock walls. "Put the greener down and fetch the doc!"

The big man in the chair eyed Longarm and Goldie suspiciously. His eyes were as gray as the window above the cluttered desk before him. He wore a fur hat from which curly, light brown hair curled. His face was the size of a serving tray and weathered as raw as the local lawman's. This man's was also bearded, with strands of gray showing among the sandy brown. Still awakening from the nap he'd apparently been enjoying, he set the greener across the desk and rose from the chair.

He kept on rising until his head would have smacked

the seven-foot ceiling if he hadn't stooped. Longarm had seen smaller bears. This man smelled like a bear, too—fresh from his den in his ratty bear coat that hung to the tops of his worn black boots.

The giant again scrutinized the newcomers, his nostrils working as though sniffing prospective prey.

"Guests, Emil," the local lawman said wryly. "We have guests."

Emil pointed at Goldie's bloody shoulder. "What happened?" he said in a voice deeper than the local lawman's. It came out like a growl, the giant sort of grunting the oddly accented words. He was likely one of the original Romanian settlers.

"Wolf-bit," Longarm said.

The giant's anvil-sized lower jaw started to sag before he caught it, his eyes brightening with apprehension as he looked at the town marshal flanking Longarm and Goldie.

"The doc, Emil!" his boss repeated.

Emil jerked with a start. He was like a mountain moving in an earthquake. He stepped wide around Longarm, Goldie, and the town marshal, keeping his eyes on Goldie as though afraid the outlaw would try to tear his throat out. He fumbled the door open and went out, drawing it closed behind him.

"What the hell is his problem?" Goldie said.

The local lawman curled his nose at the outlaw as he stepped around him and Longarm. "Shut up." Then he pulled a trapdoor up out of the floor by a metal ring. He let the door fall back flat against the floor then went over to his desk for a lamp, which was already lit.

Longarm glanced at the three- by three-foot hole in

the floor and then at the three empty jail cells at the back of the room. All the cages were empty.

"Hold on there, pard," he said to the marshal.

"It's Calvin," the man said in his rumbling, faintly raspy voice that owned not a note of conviviality. "Frank Calvin. Like I said, there'll be a full moon tonight. And this hombre's been bit by a wolf." He shook his head tightly, showing his teeth below his mustache. "There ain't no ifs, ands, or buts about it, he's goin' in the hole, like everybody else whose been wolf-bit around here. I'll let him out tomorrow morning . . . if he hasn't turned."

Goldie turned to Longarm, who'd found himself staring in hang-jawed disbelief at the town marshal of Crazy Kate, his brain slow to reassure him that his ears had indeed picked up what he thought they had. Goldie said, "He thinks I'm a fuckin' werewolf!"

Calvin stepped up beside the hole in the floor. He held the lamp in one hand. With his other hand, he held Emil's Greener, the double bores aimed at the outlaw's belly. Loudly, he clicked back one of the rabbit-ear hammers. "Get down in the hole, mister, or I'll blow you in two with both wads, which I've filled with crushed silver ore."

"Come on, Calvin," Longarm said, chuckling. "You don't really believe that shit, do you?"

Calvin looked at Goldie and wagged the barn-blaster at the hole. "Down."

"Holy shit!" Goldie said, edging up to the hole and staring into the black earth below.

When Calvin held the lamp close enough to the hole that the outlaw could see a ways down a crude wooden

ladder, Goldie stepped into the hole, turned to look up
at Longarm fatefully, then dropped his head and began
climbing down. When Goldie was out of Longarm's
sight, Calvin crouched down and ordered Goldie to step
away from the ladder. Calvin started down, facing away
from Longarm and aiming his shotgun past his feet at
Goldie.

When Calvin had disappeared into the earth beneath
the marshal's office, Longarm climbed down the rickety
ladder, as well. Cool air rife with the smell of dank
earth, stone, and mushrooms slid over him.

At the bottom, he turned away from the ladder to
see Calvin prodding Longarm's prisoner through one
of four heavy timber, iron-banded doors embedded in
an earthen wall, on the right side of a narrow corridor
that appeared to have partly caved in. The back wall
was paneled with heavy pine boards.

There was a small barred window in each heavy
door. Calvin's lamp offered the only light. It guttered
and flickered and danced shadows around the small
dungeon, showing a Windsor chair and a small wooden
table with a deck of cards on it about halfway down the
corridor.

Furnishings for a guard, most likely.

Goldie put his face up to the barred window in his
door. His voice echoed loudly, eerily around the cavern.
"Hey, you ain't gonna leave me down here in this hole
all by my lonesome, are you?"

"Someone'll be down here later tonight," Calvin told
him. "To see if you turn. If you turn, you won't need to
worry about it no more. You won't need to know about
nothin' no more. You'll buy a load of silver buckshot
an' that'll be the end of ya!"

The town marshal of Crazy Kate tossed a small box through the barred window. "Them's lucifers. To light the torch behind you with. Best keep it lit. Gets mighty cold down here."

Longarm sighed as he lifted his hat and ran a hand through his hair. "Come on, Calvin. This is craziness. You can't tell me you really expect him to turn into a werewolf. Why, those are just in fairy tales!"

There was a commotion at the top of the stairs. Longarm turned and looked up through the hole. An aged, bespectacled face peered down at him. The glasses glinted in the light from Calvin's torch.

The man who owned the face shook his head darkly. The face disappeared. Presently, a pair of brown half boots appeared on the ladder's top rung, and then a diminutive, older man in a suit and short wolf fur coat gained the cavern floor. He held a black leather kit in his gloved right hand. He looked Longarm up and down before turning to Calvin.

"Where is he?" he said with an air of reluctance.

Calvin canted his head toward the stout door before him, which hadn't yet been latched. The town marshal held a key ring in the hand he'd freed when he placed the lamp on the table. When the doctor walked up to the door, Calvin opened it, ushered him inside, and then followed him, closing the door behind him.

Longarm waited outside the cell while the doctor tended Goldie, Calvin keeping his double-barreled barn blaster aimed at the outlaw's head. Occasionally, Goldie looked up from the doctor's work on his arm to glance darkly, incredulously, at Longarm.

When the doctor had finished, he and Calvin left Goldie sitting on a cot beneath a torch slanting away from its mounting bracket. There were several more torches in a box near the cot. They sent up the odor of the coal oil they'd been soaked in.

"Longarm," Goldie said, when Calvin had closed and locked the heavy, iron-banded door. "Longarm, you ain't gonna leave me down here, are you?"

"Not much I could do about it even if I wanted to," the federal lawman said, canting his head toward Calvin. "It's his town and he's doin' me a service, puttin' you up in it."

Calvin grinned, showing those large, brown teeth of his beneath his ostentatious silver mustache.

"Come on, Long," Calvin said, canting his head toward where the small, aged doctor was climbing the ladder. "Let's go up and have a drink. Hell, I'll buy!"

A gun blasted in the office above their heads. Dust sifted from the rafters.

"*Oh, Heaven help us!*" came the doctor's passionate plea.

Chapter 8

There were two more blasts in the office above Longarm's head. He ran to the ladder, climbed, and poked his head through the hole. The office was all murky shadows, but he could see the doctor sitting on the floor a few feet from the trapdoor, to Longarm's right. He sat with his legs straight out before him. His glasses hung off of one ear.

The old pill roller was staring toward the open front door, which was filled to brimming with the back of Emil, who was extending two six-shooters in his fists and shooting up the street to the west.

Boom! Boom! Boom!

The giant turned slowly as he fired, tracking something.

Outside, a girl screamed. *Christ, was the big deputy trying to beef a female?* It wouldn't have been any crazier than anything else that Longarm had witnessed so far in Crazy Kate. He heaved himself up out of the hole and, taking his Winchester in both hands, strode to the window over the cluttered desk. At the same time, Town

Marshal Frank Calvin heaved himself up out of the hole and looked around quickly.

"Emil, what the hell you shootin' at?"

Staring out the window, Longarm saw a large, black shadow loping westward up the street, heading for the open country beyond the town. As Emil's pistols exploded again quickly, dust and snow puffed in the street a few feet behind and to one side of the wolf, whose shiny, black coat glistened in the wintery light.

"Wolf!" Emil shouted, and fired two more times before one of his pistols clacked on an empty chamber. He fired the second gun twice more before its hammer, too, clicked empty. "Wolf on a full moon night!"

As Calvin exchanged his shotgun for a Winchester rifle at the gun rack on the wall near his desk, Longarm walked over to the door and stepped outside, moving around the giant Emil and out into the street. The wolf was little more than a jouncing black speck from this distance of a hundred yards, and it was fleeing fast.

There were several more blasts from up the street, and Longarm saw at least two more men wielding rifles—shop owners, they appeared to be, in aprons and sleeve garters. A few seconds later, the wolf swung to the right and disappeared in the rocks and sage, heading in the general direction of the towering, black northern ridge that held the brooding stone convent aloft as though in offering to Heaven.

Calvin burst out of the office, shoving the giant aside with a snarl and loudly racking a shell into his Winchester's breech.

"Gone," Longarm said.

"Ran right past here!" Emil said, grunting the words as though his tongue were as thick as his hands.

Calvin lowered the rifle and looked around the street both ways, as did Longarm, noting several small pockets of folks—men and sporting women, mostly, wearing skimpy, frilly dresses—standing around outside of a couple saloons and pleasure parlors. One such group stood outside the Carpathian Mountain Saloon, kitty-corner from the marshal's office.

The general's party was there, holding drinks and cigars. Catherine Fortescue stood to one side, her fur coat hanging open to reveal her long, slender, denim-clad figure, a pistol angling up from a wide brown belt. She wasn't wearing a hat, and her rich, honey-blond hair was blowing in the chill breeze as she looked around, as wary as all the others.

Marshal Calvin stepped out into the middle of the street, swinging his head this way and that. "Did anyone get bit by that beast? Anyone?" He turned to stare eastward toward where four parlor girls stood out on the second-story balcony of an unpainted frame house on the same side of the street as the Carpathian Mountain Saloon. Three of the girls had blankets wrapped around their shoulders. They all glanced around at one another, shaking their heads.

Just then a woman yelled hoarsely, "Help! Oh, God, help—it's my little *David*!" As the woman came from around the far side of a goat pen, a black-and-white dog trailing and sniffing concernedly up at the little boy she carried in her arms, she cried, "That beast bit him in the stable! Oh, Dr. Solomon, where *are* you?"

"Here," the doctor said, walking out of the marshal's office. "I'm here, Muriel!"

Longarm followed the doctor and Marshal Calvin eastward along the street to meet the woman staggering toward them under the weight of the nine- or ten-year-old child in her arms. Emil stood in the street outside the jailhouse, reloading his pistols and looking around warily, as though for more wolves.

A frightened murmur rose, and while most people remained close to the buildings, or swung back inside them, a few walked from various quarters toward Muriel and the boy. One of these was Catherine Fortescue. She walked with long strides, swinging her arms stiffly at her sides, concern showing in her hazel eyes, the open flaps of her fur coat jostling about her legs and the tops of her black stockman's boots.

Longarm held back from the child and the boy, keeping his rifle raised in case more wolves descended on them and the group growing around them. As Catherine brushed past him, she said, "What in God's name is happening in this country?"

Longarm didn't know how to respond to that. He was as puzzled as she obviously was, so he merely caressed his Winchester's hammer and probed the breaks between the buildings up and down the street with his keen lawman's gaze. If there was one wolf, there were certainly more.

A couple of pleasure girls holding blankets or housecoats around their shoulders had gathered with Catherine and Calvin around Muriel and the boy, who was laid out on his back in the street now while the doctor checked him over. Longarm could hear the boy whimpering. He couldn't see much of the child through the people around him, but he saw his worn, manure-crusted boots moving. He was alive, anyway.

An old, gray-haired couple stood over Muriel, who knelt beside her boy, opposite the doctor and Catherine.

The man and his wife both wore aprons, which likely meant they owned one of the near shops. There was an Old World air about them. Suddenly, one of the doxies, a pale, pudgy redhead swaddled in several ratty blankets, turned to the old folks and said, "See what you've done now? This is all your fault—I hope you know that! Now you've gone and killed Muriel's boy! You and that damn curse you brought with you from wherever in hell you come from!"

"*Opal!*" One of the other pleasure girls admonished her, shocked.

"Oh, God!" Opal cried, pressing her hands to her face. "Why didn't I get the hell out of here while I had the chance? Oh, Christ—now it's winter and I'll be here till spring with these crazy, evil people!"

Something moved in the corner of Longarm's right eye. He swung around to see a gray wolf sticking its head out of a break between the whorehouse and a feed store. Longarm raised the Winchester, raking back the hammer, aimed, and fired just as the beast pulled its head into the break.

The lawman's bullet plowed up sand and gravel a few feet inside the break as the rifle's report flattened out across the street and echoed off the steep canyon walls. The echo hadn't died before a long, mournful, menacing wolf's howl replaced it. Only half-aware of doing it, Longarm ran across the street and into the break between the buildings.

Beyond the other end of the alley, he could see the wolf running off through the sage and rocks, swerving to avoid a small log cabin to which a stable was attached. The animal disappeared in a gully for a few seconds, and then Longarm saw the beast again, climbing a low, rocky hill. There was another one with it now, just a little lighter gray than the first one.

Several yards beyond the cabin, Longarm stopped. The two wolves stopped at the top of the hill and looked back at him, their tongues hanging. They seemed to be smiling. Longarm raised the rifle though he knew they were too far away now for an accurate shot, and he fired once anyway.

The bullet merely snapped a branch from a small sage shrub as the two wolves continued running and dropped out of sight down the hill's opposite side. Longarm cursed as he ejected the spent cartridge, heard it clink off a rock behind him, then levered a fresh round into the Winchester's breech.

He'd just set the hammer to half cock and was turning back toward the main street when he saw a figure standing in the open back door of the whorehouse—a woman with rich, dark hair piled atop her head. Longarm thought she was in her late twenties, early thirties. She wore a gold-speckled red vest over a loose white blouse, and several pleated wool skirts. She leaned against the door frame, arms crossed as she smoked a long, thin cigar. Her brown-eyed face owned an open, earthy beauty. She didn't seem worried about the wolves, but merely amused by them.

Smiling at Longarm, she shook her head dubiously and drew deep on the cigar.

Longarm lowered the rifle and walked slowly toward her. When he was a few feet away, he saw that she was pretty, though not in a painted-girl kind of way. This woman might run the place, but she herself wasn't for sale. She wore no face paint. There were a few strands of gray in her brown hair. Her frank, amused gaze seemed to communicate more than Longarm could understand, as though she had a secret she was fond of not sharing. It troubled him.

"Who're you?"

The woman shook her head, let her eyes rake him up and down. Her breasts were full behind the loose cotton blouse that she wore open to the top of her deep cleavage. "Who're *you*?"

"You first."

The woman laughed raspily at his response and then changed the subject. "How's Mrs. Leonard's boy?"

"I—"

"Longarm?"

He turned to see Catherine standing at the mouth of the alley through which he'd followed the wolf. She looked harried, worried. "Custis, please don't let Marshal Calvin lock that poor boy up in his cellar! For Christ's sake, that's what he *intends*!"

Longarm glanced at the dark-eyed woman, who was still smiling condescendingly at the federal lawman. "Yes, that's what he intends, and that's what he'll do," she said with a nod. "It's a full moon night, don't ya know!"

Longarm still wanted to know who she was, but she could wait. He turned away from her and walked over to where Catherine waited for him, glancing curiously behind him at the dark-eyed woman in the gold-speckled vest. "Who's she?"

Longarm shook his head as he continued past Catherine to stride through the break between buildings toward the main street. He was aware again of the long, mournful, menacing cry of the wolf—the same one he'd heard just after he'd taken the shot at the gray wolf earlier. It seemed to be originating high above the town, from either the southern or the northern cliff. From the echoes, it was hard to tell.

The convent?

He shook his head at the half-formed, half-conscious question and walked out of the break and into the street, where Marshal Frank Calvin was holding the wolf-bit boy in his arms. The boy's mother, Muriel Leonard, knelt before Calvin, steepling her hands in front of her chest, begging. She and Dr. Solomon were the only people with the town marshal now—besides the giant Emil, of course, who stood awkwardly near Calvin, holding his two pistols straight down at his sides. The pistols looked little larger than derringers in his huge brown hands.

The doctor stood behind the woman, his hands on her arms as though trying to help her rise.

"You know the rules, Mrs. Leonard," Calvin was saying in a loud but patient voice, the boy sobbing and stretching a mittened hand out toward his mother. There was a splotch of blood across his belly, inside the right flap of his brown wool coat. He wore wool trousers the same color as the coat and the worn, manure-crusted boots.

"Please, Marshal Calvin—I beg you!" Muriel Thompson was howling. "Don't take my boy to that cellar. Don't take him! Oh, don't take him! *Pleeeease!*"

"Oh, for Christ sakes," Catherine said, moving up to stand beside the pleading woman, glaring at Calvin, her fists on her hips. "How can you possibly throw an injured little boy in a *cellar*?"

Calvin parried the woman's hard stare with a hard

one of his own. "You stay out of this, Miss whoever-the-hell-you are!"

"Calvin!" Longarm said. "Have you gone *mad*?"

"You, too, Mr. Federal Lawman! You two ain't *from* here. You got no business pokin' your noses in!"

Mrs. Leonard looked at Longarm, tears streaming down her cheeks. "Oh, please, Marshal—please don't let him take my David to the Wolf Hold!"

"Wolf Hold?" Longarm said, unbelievingly. "That's what you call that hole in there?"

"Long," Calvin said, tightening his jaws and flaring his nostrils, "I'm warnin' you to stay out of this town's business!"

Just then the giant Emil lifted the two guns in his hands and aimed them at Longarm. The giant curled one corner of his thick-lipped mouth, and his eyes went hard as granite. The pistols held unwaveringly on Longarm.

"Step back," Calvin said, glancing at Catherine. "Both of you."

Longarm glanced once more at the giant's pistols aimed at his belly. Catherine looked up at Longarm, her hazel eyes stricken. Longarm held his rifle in his right hand on his shoulder. He wrapped his left hand around Catherine's arm and pulled her a couple of steps back behind him.

Meanwhile, the boy continued crying for his mother, while Mrs. Leonard lowered her head and sobbed.

"He'll be all right, Muriel," the doctor said to her gently. "I'll see to that. I'll see that his wound is tended and that he's fed and kept warm. It's only for a few hours, until the moon has set."

Calvin began turning toward the marshal's office, cutting a sharp glance at his big deputy still aiming the pistols. "Stay here and guard the door, Emil," Calvin ordered. "Anyone tries to get into my office without my permission, shoot him." He looked at Catherine. "Or her."

To Mrs. Leonard, he said, "As soon as I have David secured, you can come down and see him. Hell, I'll even let you stay with him." Then he looked at the doctor and canted his head toward the door. "Doc!"

When Calvin and the doctor had gone into the marshal's office and closed the door behind them, leaving Mrs. Leonard kneeling in the street, sobbing with her head down, Longarm looked again at Emil. The giant sidestepped over to the marshal's office door and stood in front of it, making it obvious that anyone intending to enter the office would have to go through him. Through him and the two cocked Remington pistols in his hands, that was.

"I'm sorry, Mrs. Leonard," Catherine said, kneeling beside the crying woman. "I'm so sorry. At least the marshal is going to let you see little David soon."

"I shouldn't have let him muck out the stable," the woman said through her cries, shaking her head, shoulders quivering. "I shouldn't have let him outside with so many wolves prowling around!"

"I'll take care of her." This from behind Longarm and Catherine. Both turned to see the woman whom Longarm had been eyeing a few minutes ago, in the back doorway of the whorehouse. She stood now in a quilted deerskin coat, looking between Longarm and Catherine and Mrs. Leonard. She stepped forward and placed her hands on the woman's shoulders.

"Come, Muriel," she said. "We'll go inside your house, and I'll fix us both some tea. I'll add a shot of brandy. Take the edge off." As Mrs. Leonard rose, wiping the tears from her cheeks with the backs of her hands, she turned to look up at the dark-eyed woman before her. "Oh, Zeena, I don't know what I'm going to do. David is all I have. You don't think . . . don't think . . . ?" Her eyes were bright with horror.

"Shh, it's going to be all right," Zeena said, beginning to lead Muriel away. "I doubt very much that he's cursed, Muriel. It's such a rare, rare thing!"

"Oh, but what if he *does turn?*"

When they'd walked off down the street and turned to head to Mrs. Leonard's house off the street's north side, Longarm glanced at Emil, who stood like a giant statue in front of the door, boots spread a little more than shoulder width apart. He held the Remingtons crossed on his chest. His cold, gray eyes bored into Longarm.

Catherine looked at the giant, too, and sighed. She swung her head toward Longarm, turning her mouth corners down in silent, helpless exasperation. "Buy you a drink?" She canted her head toward the Carpathian Mountain Saloon.

Longarm glanced at Emil and then turned to Catherine. "Why the hell not?"

Chapter 9

Longarm tipped his bottle of Maryland rye to one side and watched the honey-brown liquid run out of the bottle's neck. It hit the deep valley between Catherine Fortescue's breasts and splashed up against the side of each. The splashes were little larger than freckles.

Goose bumps rose on them.

Her nipples pebbled.

"Oh!" the young woman groaned as she lay on her back in her room in the Carpathian Hotel. She shivered delightedly, lifting one bare knee and then the other. "Oh, God, that's incredible!"

She was holding Longarm's fully erect cock in her left hand, pumping him slowly. Longarm turned the bottle up and then lowered his head to the girl's belly, watching the whiskey run down the valley between her breasts and across her belly to pool in her belly button. As it did, quickly filling the dimple, he dipped his tongue in it and then slurped it up.

"Ahh . . . *Christ!*" Catherine cried tensing her jaws and squirming around, releasing his cock to press both hands to his head as he ran his tongue up north of her belly button, following the trail of liquor, to her breasts.

She giggled, grunted, groaned, arched her back as his tongue very slowly made the journey. Just below her breasts that jutted like pale, pink-tipped mountains, he glanced up to see that chicken flesh stood out on nearly every inch of her torso. Her nipples jutted, hard as thimbles.

Longarm smiled and continued sliding his tongue up between her breasts to the point where the whiskey had dropped onto her. Lapped up off the girl's sweet body, the tanglefoot tasted like honey. A nice contrast to the sweetness was the burn at the back of his tongue and in his throat.

Another nice contrast was the slick wetness he felt against his left middle finger, which he had inserted into the delicate, petal-like folds of her pussy, flicking it up and down and sideways and in and out. That caused her to groan and grind her thighs together.

When Longarm pulled his finger out of the lightly furred portal of her core, she sighed and drew a long, deep breath.

He smacked his lips together. "Tasty."

"Come down here," she said, wrapping her arms around his neck and drawing his lips down to hers. They kissed hungrily, entangling each other's tongue. With his left hand, he kneaded her breasts, flicking her nipples with his thumb.

It was a nice reprieve from the craziness of all that had come in the hours before.

When Longarm had stabled his and Goldie's mounts

in the nearest livery barn, he'd met Catherine at the saloon, and they'd come directly to her room, using the rear steps climbing to a second-story door, to avoid the girl's father and the rest of her hunting party. Not that she cared what any of them thought about her dalliances with the federal lawman—and Longarm saw that the general had little say in his hot-blooded daughter's doings—but she'd said they were all drunk and getting loud and full of tiresome braggadocio, making plans to stalk and kill the wolf who'd leaped on Murphy's travois and dragged the poor, wounded man off so quickly that there'd been nothing the others could do about it.

"He was just gone, so suddenly gone," Catherine had told Longarm while they undressed together quickly as soon as they walked into her room. "And then more wolves were running toward us, so we had to leave him there, his screams dying oh so slowly."

Desperately seeking distraction, she'd dropped to her knees in front of Longarm, dug his cock out of his balbriggans, and sucked him so dry that he didn't think he'd have another drop of jism to ejaculate for a month.

Now they mashed their hot tongues together. As he pulled his head back from hers, her tongue followed his out of her mouth, and they separated. She rose onto her elbows, grabbed the bottle off the nightstand, and took a long, manlike pull, wiping her rich, red lips with the back of her hand.

She narrowed one eye speculatively and smiled, her hazel eyes flashing in the gray afternoon light pushing through a near window. "I think I'd like to fuck one more time, Custis. Can we do that before we begin thinking again about the wolves and that poor David Leonard in Marshal Calvin's cellar?"

"Fine as frog hair." Longarm rolled the girl onto her belly, Catherine laughing, her delightful breasts jostling. "I'd like a better angle this time," he said, and holding her up against his hips with his right arm, he slowly impaled her with his jutting shaft.

"Uh, *God!*" she groaned, grabbing the bed's brass frame as though it were the rail of a storm-thrashed ship.

He hammered her hard for nearly fifteen minutes, sweating, the bedsprings sighing in accompaniment to her groans and muffled cries. In and out, in and out. His cock seemed to grow and grow. Her snatch expanded and contracted like a hand wringing out a rag . . . until he drew her hard against him one last time and, arching his back and thrusting his pelvis forward, gave himself to the spasming release.

His burly grunt echoed off the wooden walls.

Catherine released the bed frame. She dropped like so much wet wash from a line, her head coming to rest on a pillow, her ass still drawn up hard against Longarm's shaft that was only just now beginning to dwindle.

"Mr. Lawman, sir," she said in a rich, breathy voice, "you sure can fuck."

Outside, a wolf howled. Long and mournful. Longarm froze, listening. Something told him it was the same wolf he'd heard before—the one that seemed to be on a high perch above the town.

He removed his arm from around Catherine's waist, and her hips sagged down against the bed. She rolled onto her side and drew her knees toward her breasts as she watched him climb down off the bed, his pecker lightly slapping his thigh as he moved to the window over the washstand.

"What do you suppose he wants?" she said, still a little breathless, sweeping her thick hair back behind her ear. "More blood?"

Longarm remembered what Goldie had told him about the woman, Crazy Kate, who'd been locked up in the convent perched high on that pinnacle of rock. Just like before, he suppressed the nonsensical possibility that the howls could belong to the woman, and looked up and down the street.

The sky was gray. Snow fell from it lazily, dusting the tan ground. Straight up, however, the clouds were parting. The light was fading at the end of a late-autumn day high in the San Juans. The moon would be rising soon.

The full moon.

It appeared that so far no wolves prowled the streets. But what would happen when darkness fell? Longarm hoped all the residents of Crazy Kate had strong doors and windows. Likely, they did. He had a feeling the current plethora of wolves around here was not a recent occurrence. Something told him the village had been living with this many critters for months. Maybe years.

He grabbed the whiskey bottle, took a pull.

Catherine reached out from the bed, wrapped her hand around his slack dong, running a thumb over the head. "I love your cock."

"My cock loves you."

"Could we stay right here and fuck the rest of the day and night away?"

Longarm took another pull from the bottle and

shook his head as he continued staring into the street, shuttling his gaze to the marshal's office. Calvin's two front windows were lit against the coming darkness. "I'm gonna see about my prisoner and the boy. I'd best check around to see if there's any human wolves on the prowl out there . . . along with the four-legged brand."

"Human wolves?"

"Goldie and his bunch had been aimin' to meet up with some of their former gang members up here in the mountains somewhere. I don't know where exactly. Somethin' tells me they probably know by now what happened to three of their ilk back at Hawk's Bluff, and that Goldie is here."

"You think they'll try to bust him out of Calvin's Wolf Hold?"

"Hope so. I might as well haul their asses back to Denver along with Goldie's. Just as soon not have to come back here anytime soon."

She brushed her fingers along the underside of his scrotum. "After all the fun we've had?"

Longarm shuddered to the thrill of her touch. He snorted and sat down on the bed. He handed her the bottle. She drank. When she was through, he leaned down and, cupping her right breast, kissed the nipple of the other one. She ran her hands through his hair, lightly raked her fingers across his unshaven jaw.

"I'm gonna go out have me a talk with Calvin, see how deep this werewolf idea goes," he said, rising and reaching for his clothes.

She threw the covers back. "Can I come with you?"

He looked at her lying naked and semi-curled on the bed, her young, taut body long-legged, firm-busted, and ripe. Her eyes were coy, playful as she stared up from beneath her brows, her beautiful face exquisitely framed by her love-tangled hair. Her cheeks were flushed with fulfillment.

Longarm sighed. "Has any man ever been able to say no to you, Catherine?"

She grinned, got up, and started washing herself at the stand beneath the window. They both froze for a second when the wolf howled again.

Longarm and Catherine left the room together, their boots clomping on the second-story floorboards.

As Catherine gave him one last peck on the cheek and started down the stairs, Longarm paused to dig a three-for-a-nickel cheroot out of his shirt pocket and light it. He puffed on it for a while, rolling it expertly between his lips, savoring the honey-like taste of the girl and the whiskey lingering on his tongue and now mixing with the peppery, woodsy taste of the smoke. From below rose a cloud of tobacco smoke and the low rumble of conversation as well as the clinking of glasses and bottles.

Longarm saw that the Carpathian was teeming with clientele—mostly bearded locals in suspenders, dungarees, and cone-shaped, floppy-brimmed hats or watch caps, but with several non-native shopkeepers and cowpunchers from area ranches thrown in, as well. The punchers were probably in town to wait out the long winter before roundup and the resumption of steady pay.

The general's men, conspicuous in their ostentatious frontier garb—fringed buckskin slacks and tunics decorated every which way with beads and fake

porcupine quills—sat in the middle of the milling
crowd. They were a raucous quartet, and the general
was just now standing with his arm around a bare-
breasted, bored-looking Indian whore and gesturing
wildly while speaking to a bearded local at the table
next to his own.

"Strychnine!" the general said, poking his cigar at
the man to whom he spoke. "You people get a wagon-
load of strychnine up here and toss it into the woods
around the town. Hell, poison all the trash heaps. Now,
you might kill a few dogs and coyotes"—the general
laughed, taking several puffs from his cigar—"but I
guarantee you'll solve your wolf problem in a matter
of days!"

One of his friends, who resembled Buffalo Bill in
his gray-streaked blond muttonchops and goatee,
climbed wobbly footed from his chair and announced
as though to the entire room, "And I, Hiriam H. R.
Langeford the Fourth, here and now promise to pay for
the entire load—wagon, driver, and as much poison as
it takes to expunge your furry menace from these
environs!"

A tall, gangly puncher got up and whooped, waving
his hat in the air. Several of the painted girls milling
about the room clapped. One stuck two fingers in her
mouth and whistled.

"Thank you, sir!" This from the bartender, a middle-
aged man in a beard but with a clean-shaven upper lip.
He had a heavy Old World accent, and he continued
with what Longarm detected in his overloud voice to
be irony: "That will certainly take care of our problem.
Indeed!" He looked at several of the other native locals
sitting about the room in their suspenders and smoking

their pipes, looking bored with the moneyed gents' car-ryings-on. "Won't it, my brothers?"

The men he'd spoken to merely smiled fatefully and shook their heads. One raised his beer schooner to the barman, turned his mouth corners down, and drank as though to a dark fate, a cold grave.

Chapter 10

Longarm felt a knot grow behind his belt buckle as, descending the stairs, he looked around at the locals and then at the more recent settlers of Crazy Kate, who were mostly younger and without that dark, Old World cynicism in their gazes. He looked at the general now, and the contrast was even starker as the man turned to his daughter, wobbling drunkenly, the pretty Indian doxie holding him up, one arm wrapped around his considerable waist, the other hand splayed on his chest.

Her small breasts jostled as she moved with the old, drunk soldier.

"Catherine, my dear. So good of you to join us. I was getting worried." The general looked at Longarm and grinned devilishy. "Fornicating again, my dear?" he asked his daughter. "Whatever will I do with you?"

"The apple doesn't fall far from the tree, does it, Father?" Catherine said, stopping and hiking an elbow atop the bar. She nodded at the Indian girl. "You pay her well. She's gonna earn every penny."

Catherine glanced at Longarm, who bellied up to the bar beside her.

With the help of the Indian girl, General Fortescue wended his way through the tables and chairs and approached his daughter and the tall federal lawman, who had just ordered a drink for him and her. He'd been intending on heading over to the town marshal's office, but he saw Marshal Frank Calvin just now entering the Carpathian Mountain, batting his hat against his thigh to dislodge the fresh dusting of snow.

Flanking him, the saloon's large window was fading to lilac, snow pellets flecking the glass.

The general said, "Marshal Long, I must say I'm surprised but pleased to see you here. The wolves were absolutely devilish along the trail. I take it Catherine informed you about what happened to one of our party?" The general cleared his throat and grinned with half of his mouth mantled with the thick, silver walrus mustache. "I assume you two do talk *some* . . ."

"Some," Catherine said, taking the glass from her father's hand and skidding it across the bar.

"She did," Longarm said. "My condolences, General."

"Imagine these people believing in werewolves!"

"It's true, mister." This from Frank Calvin walking up behind the general with his long, wool-lined deerskin coat hanging open.

"Uh . . . that's General Fortescue," said his bodyguard, Captain Sidney Ashton-Green, who'd been slowly, not inconspicuously gravitating toward Catherine since she'd dropped down out of her and Longarm's love nest on the second story.

"Oh, that's quite all right, Sidney," the general said,

extending his hand toward the town marshal. "Marshal, I don't believe we've been formally introduced."

Calvin scowled back at the rotund ex-soldier, the town marshal's eyes critically raking the general's flashy buckskin attire. Reluctantly, he shook the man's hand, not bothering to remove his glove. "Frank Calvin, General. How long do you and your people figure on stayin' here in Crazy Kate? Winter's comin' on, don't you know. The passes will have you all sealed in soon." He narrowed an eye at Longarm. "You, too, Marshal Long."

"Kind of hard to leave now, isn't it," said Captain Ashton-Green, "with so many wolves on the prowl? The general and myself and our compadres have decided to head out first thing in the morning and shoot as many as we can."

"Yes," said General Fortescue, lifting his chin and throwing his shoulders back, though the Indian girl had to lean into him hard to steady him, "we'll be bringing back enough pelts by sundown tomorrow to provide winter coats for everyone residing in your fair town for quite some time. Might not get them all, but enough to scare the others away."

"Ah, never thought of that," said Calvin with a wry glance at the bartender.

"My associate, Mr. Langeford over there"—the general canted his head toward the goat-bearded dandy who sat sleeping in his chair, amid a plethora of empty bottles, shot glasses, and beer mugs—"has promised to send up a wagon loaded with arsenic. That should solve the problem straightaway. I suggest you keep a good supply of the poison on hand. A great many wolves do seem attracted to this neck of the mountains, for some odd reason."

"Ah, hell," the barman intoned in his heavy, Eastern European brogue, scowling toward the front of the saloon. "I forgot to close the shutters on the place, and here the sun is nearly down!" He added a couple of what sounded like expletives in his native tongue and then, glancing worriedly at Calvin, scrambled out from around the bar, heading for the front door.

Catherine glanced worriedly at Longarm. "Don't worry," he said beneath the crowd's low roar. "They wouldn't . . ."

He let his voice trail off as he looked at the window and saw two yellow eyes, like miniature lanterns, glowing just beyond the glass. Wolf shadows danced around behind the eyes. Longarm's pulse hammered. He shuttled his gaze to the bartender, who was just now walking out the front door.

Longarm jerked forward, sliding his Colt from its holster. "Hold on, mister!"

Too late.

The barman had no sooner stepped out onto the Carpathian Mountain's front porch than he screamed as he swung to his left and a heavy, dark figure leaped onto him. Just as the barman struck the porch floor, the two yellow eyes beyond the glass moved upward, and suddenly a huge, black wolf was leaping through the window in a hail of breaking glass.

A whore screamed. A man yelled. The crowd turned toward the front of the saloon as though all heads were attached to the same rope.

Glass shattered and rained on the floor with a sound like ten babies screeching. Out of the curtain of spraying glass, the wolf leaped onto the far end of the bar, back humped, head down, hackles raised, fangs bared.

The beast looked around quickly and, finding a victim sitting nearby, had just started to leap, when Longarm's Colt spoke twice.

The beast screeched and did a sort of pirouette in midair. It fell against a man smoking a pipe, throwing the man out of his chair and piling up on top of him while everyone nearby leaped away.

Longarm saw another wolf leaping through the window, and fired. The wolf yipped and hit the floor behind the bar.

Frank Calvin was running up behind Longarm, yelling, "Oh, Jesus Christ! Jesus Christ!"

Longarm dashed to the window, his Colt extended and ready to fire, broken glass crunching beneath his boots. He looked through what remained of the window.

No other wolves were in view until he'd stepped through the window and turned to see three beasts attacking the bartender, who cowered and screamed, kicking and trying to shield his head and face with his hands. Blood spurted in all directions, staining the saloon's front doors and the porch floor.

Longarm lunged forward, stopped, took careful aim, and fired. One of the wolves—a wiry gray— screamed, twisted around, and rolled up against the porch rail, biting at its bullet-torn right side. The others were jouncing around so wildly that Longarm's next two rounds merely punched holes in the porch floor. The wolves barked, snarled, and either ran down the front steps or leaped over the rail, and quickly disappeared into the snowy blue gloaming.

"Ah, hell." Marshal Calvin stood in the open saloon door, looking down at the apron-clad barman writhing in a growing pool of his own blood. He convulsed violently, dying fast.

Across the street, a gun flashed, the roar of the shotgun's two barrels reaching Longarm's ears a quarter second later. The giant deputy, Emil, stood just outside the jailhouse, aiming the gut-shredder at the fleeing wolves, who were long out of range of the pellet-pusher.

Emil lowered the shotgun, broke it open, and hurriedly began replacing the spent loads with fresh. Longarm reloaded his Colt as he moved down off the Carpathian's porch steps, looking carefully up and down the street. Calvin followed him out, extending two cocked pistols.

"Your wolves are mighty brave, Marshal," Longarm said as he walked up the street a few feet and peered into the gap between the saloon and the building beside it—a harness shop over which was perched Dr. Solomon's office.

"They ain't *my* wolves—I'll tell you that." Calvin triggered his pistol into the wolf now lying dead against the porch rail. He fired again, causing the animal to jerk.

"What's that for?" Longarm asked, satisfied that no wolves were lurking in the break between the saloon and the harness shop.

"I'm loaded with silver." Calvin turned and walked back into the saloon that was buzzing with nervous chatter as the drinkers and cardplayers milled around to inspect the two dead wolves.

Calvin was inside only a few seconds before two pistol shots echoed inside the place. A girl gasped with a start. Then Calvin walked out the front door, plucking the spent cartridges from one of his pistols and muttering, "Gave them a little dollop of silver, too."

"Werewolves, you think?" Longarm said, ironically, as he peered down the gap along the saloon's opposite side.

"That's what I think, all right." Calvin looked at Emil, who stood in the middle of the street, turning slowly, aiming his shotgun straight out from his right shoulder, ready for another onslaught. "Emil, hitch up a wagon. You an' me are gonna haul these critters off, show the others what happens when they get as brave as they're gettin' tonight."

"Come on, Marshal," Catherine said, standing in the open saloon door, her pistol in her hand. "You don't really believe this werewolf legend, do you?"

"Sure enough I do. I've seen a man turn, had to put him down like a rabid . . . well, wolf. This didn't just start, neither. The Wolf Hold under the jailhouse was built nigh on twenty years ago, when a boy named Anatol Moldova was killed by a werewolf. That wolf bit someone else that same night—a prospector named Henri Conanda. Conanda came to town sick as hell. The doc fixed him up, sent him home, and the next full moon old Conanda returned to town, demanding to be locked up. He said the moon was makin' him crazy."

Longarm stood off the saloon's east front corner, his pistol down, watching the silver-mustached lawman, who stood now over the dead barman lying near the wolf that, in turn, lay against the porch rail.

Calvin said, "The marshal at the time locked him up, had to kill him that night. He said Conanda turned, all right, and was about to break out the jailhouse door. The marshal shot him with a silver bullet."

"Just had a few of those layin' around, did he?" Catherine asked.

"Yep. The marshal himself was from the Old Country, and suspected that he and the others who'd settled here had brought the werewolf curse with them from the Romanian mountains. He was ready. Good thing he was. After that night, he set to work digging that Wolf Hold and installin' them cells. Since then, anyone bit by a wolf around here is locked up over the time of the full moon . . . just in case they turn."

Longarm and Catherine shared a look.

He asked Calvin, "How many have turned?"

"Enough to make me not wanna fuck around, time o' the full moon." Calvin glanced at Catherine standing behind him. "Do pardon my French, miss."

"Of course."

"You'd best get on inside," Calvin told her, closing the front door on her and then going over and closing the large shutter over the broken front window. He looked down at the dead barman. "Mr. Korga got careless. Damn careless. Most folks around here don't forget when there's a full moon."

"I reckon they wouldn't," Longarm said, scratching his head, thoroughly befuddled. He didn't know what to believe or not to believe. But he couldn't believe in werewolves until he actually saw a man turn into one, and that hadn't happened yet.

A loud rattling sounded up the street. Longarm looked that way, to see Emil hoorawing a horse pulling a box wagon toward him and Marshal Calvin.

When Emil had reined the wagon to a stop in front of the saloon, the giant climbed down. Longarm stood watch in the street while the local lawmen carried the dead barman, Korga, down off the porch and set him in the wagon. They then dragged the two wolves out of the saloon and tossed them into the back of the wagon, as well. When they'd loaded the one from the porch, Emil climbed back into the driver's boot, causing the carriage to jerk and squawk under his enormous weight.

Calvin turned to Longarm. "We'll take Korga over to the undertaker then haul these dead critters off a ways. Seein' what happened to these three might warn the others. Likely not, but hell, who knows?"

"Yeah, who knows?"

"Will you watch over the jailhouse till I come back?"

"Why not?"

Calvin offered a grim smile. "Just in case you feel like turnin' that boy loose"—the town marshal patted his coat pocket—"I got the key."

He pinched his hat brim and glanced at Emil. The giant shook the reins over the horse's back, and they rocked and rattled eastward along the main street, disappearing into the quickly thickening night.

Longarm looked up at the rising moon. He felt himself grimace.

Were Goldie and the boy about to turn into werewolves?

He scoffed at the notion. He didn't like that it didn't seem a genuine, heartfelt scoff.

Chapter 11

Longarm retrieved his rifle from his room and came back downstairs, where the drinkers were reveling as they had been before the wolves had come knocking. He had a feeling the revelry was a full moon tradition—a time when everyone in town got together for safety and to distract themselves from the savagery.

It was a dark festival time . . .

Another bartender had been called up from one of the whorehouses, on his day off, to fill in for the one who'd nearly been devoured by the wolves. This one was a rangy, retired ranch foreman with coal-black hair and mustache but with a face as wizened as an ancient, work-worn glove. He also had a limp, and he was limping up and down the bar now, filling drink orders, as Longarm wended his way through the crowd to the front.

Catherine intercepted him, putting a hand on his arm and glancing back at her father and the other men in their hunting party. "Custis, you have to do something. You heard what my father said earlier—about hunting down the wolves? Well, it turns out he means it. I thought he was just drunk, but I can tell now they've worked themselves up over this."

"You don't think after the drinks wear off and the hangovers kick in they'll have a change of heart . . . and head?"

Catherine shook her head at the men now playing cards at their table. The Indian girl was sitting on the lap of one of the other men, and she was casting fearful looks toward the front of the room. She was one of the few for whom the wolves had seemed to temper the evening's pleasure.

"No," Catherine said. "These are prideful men. They intend to ride out and hunt down the wolves, because they boasted they'd do so to the whole town. The fools. They're underequipped. All except father are underskilled. Father's just too damn old to be out there. By morning, they might want to call the hunt off, but they won't."

"What do you want me to do?"

"Try to reason with them. They might listen to you, you being a man. They won't listen to me. They think I'm insulting their manhood." Catherine made a disgusted face, crossing her arms on her breasts and shaking her head. "Men."

"Yeah, well, I have to go watch the jailhouse while Calvin and his deputy dump the dead wolves somewhere. When I come back, I'll have a talk with the general, though I don't know what good it'll do."

"Thank you." Catherine kissed his cheek, gave him a smoky, sexy look. "Be careful out there. When you come back, I'll try to have a bath waiting for us. Going to be a cold night."

Longarm grinned and glanced at the ceiling. "Not up there."

She lowered her perfect chin and winked. "Nope."

Longarm went out, closing the doors tightly behind him. He stepped over the blood left by the barman Korga and the wolf. The moon was on the rise in the southeast, flashing dully behind scudding clouds.

He glanced over at the jailhouse. A lamp shone in the window. He was reluctant to go over there, as he knew he was going to feel like an accessory to jailing the poor Leonard boy, and he had no way of springing him.

He sighed and reached inside his sheepskin to dig a three-for-a-nickel cheroot out of the breast pocket of his frock coat. He lit up, glanced at the moon again, and looked up and down the street through the wafting smoke, wondering what all this meant—the wolves, the Wolf Hold, the idea that at least some of the wolves were supernatural. He knew such talk was blarney, but he also knew he couldn't entirely reject the idea.

Someone had gone to a lot of work to dig that hole beneath the jailhouse floor. And Calvin and at least several of the locals here in Crazy Kate just seemed so damned *convinced*.

The howl from high above dropped down like some mournful call from Heaven. It was a long, slightly high-pitched cry, the lament of a lonely she-bitch, maybe, and it echoed for a long time around this deep canyon, around the town, before it died slowly. When silence had returned once more, Longarm realized that his knees were warm. Sort of spongy. He felt a little like he'd felt back home in West-by-God-Virginia, when he'd been listening to the old people gathered around telling stories about the mountain hoodoo spirits.

Damn, this town was getting to him.

He drew deep on the cigar and then removed it from between his lips, blew out the smoke, and, holding his rifle low but ready in his right hand, dropped down off the porch steps and into the street. He angled toward the jailhouse and the dull light in its uncurtained window. He was halfway there when something ripped into the street just right of his right boot, lifting an angry *whomp!*

The rifle's report banged out from above and behind Longarm a half second later. In the corner of his right eye, he'd seen the flash. Now he hurled himself left, hit the ground on his right shoulder, raised his own Winchester, and fired twice quickly at a man-shaped silhouette perched atop the hardware store directly behind him.

The silhouette pulled back behind the roof's lip as Longarm's first slug clipped the edge of a shake shingle, ripping it out of the roof, and his second bullet sailed toward a star flickering behind scudding clouds.

Keeping his eyes on the hardware store roof, Longarm heaved himself to his feet. The silhouette appeared once more—a hatted head, a pair of shoulders, and a rifle—and Longarm swung to his left and ran full out toward a stock trough fronting a barbershop. The bushwhacker's rifle ripped two more chunks of dirt and horseshit out of the street perilously close to Longarm's scissoring legs, and one more hammered the stock trough as the federal lawman bounded off his heels and vaulted over the trough to hit the frozen ground behind it hard enough to rattle his brains and lift a cat squeal in his ears.

Longarm chomped down hard against the pain in his right shoulder, hipped around, and edged a look over the top of the stock trough. The silhouette was still visible above the lip of the hardware store roof. The man had his cheek pressed up taut against his rifle stock.

Longarm jerked his head down in time for the bushwhacker's next bullet to miss his skull by literally a hairsbreadth—he felt the bullet's hot breath across the top of his scalp, parting his close-cropped hair, before it hammered an upright of the hitch rack behind him.

Longarm glanced over the stock trough. The bushwhacker had raised his rifle to cock it. Quickly, Longarm raised his own Winchester once more, resting the barrel atop the trough, and fired three quick rounds, triggering and levering, hearing the spent casings clinking against the barbershop's stone porch pylons behind him.

He held fire, squinted through his own wafting powder smoke as the ambusher's silhouette sort of jerked back from the roof's lip, threw an arm out for balance to keep from falling, and then scrambled back away from the edge.

"You think you're runnin' away, now, eh, you son of a bitch?" Longarm ground his jaws in rage as he scrambled to his feet, replacing the cartridges he'd fired with fresh from his cartridge belt. He ran straight across the street and into an alley mouth, hoping to catch the bushwhacker climbing down off the roof of the hardware store. He kicked an empty airtight tin, cursed, and kept on running before he slowed as he approached the store's rear.

Holding the Winchester high and barrel-up, he edged a look around the corner just as a figure dropped down from the roof and toward a loose, cone-shaped pile of split firewood. When the ambusher was six feet from the ground, he triggered his rifle, the gun stabbing a knife-shaped flame toward Longarm, the slug plowing into the rear of the hardware store, six inches from Longarm's nose.

The lawman lurched back, raking out a curse but also impressed by the killer's instincts, knowing where Longarm would be and when.

The bushwhacker landed atop the woodpile with a clattering thump and a grunt. Longarm stepped out away from the building's corner, aiming the Winchester straight out from his right hip. The bushwhacker was scrambling down the far side of the woodpile, throwing one arm and his rifle out for balance.

Longarm's Winchester roared, but the bushwhacker bounded behind a low shed on the far side of the woodpile, and Longarm's bullet barked into the shed's near wall. Longarm racked a fresh round and paused, holding his position, aiming the rifle at the shed.

Silence.

Nothing moved.

The man must be holed up on the far side of the shed.

The shed was a chicken coop with a steeply pitched roof, the low part facing Longarm. He looked at the woodpile and then at the chicken coop roof, judging the distance. He drew a deep breath, ran forward, climbed the woodpile in two swift bounds, and propelled himself from the top and onto the roof of the coop. He landed on his hands and knees then lurched forward, two more strides taking him to the steepest part of the roof, where he could look down over the opposite side.

The man-shaped shadow holding a rifle lurched back away from the wall, the rifle barrel jerking up toward

Longarm. The federal lawmen yelled, "Halt!" only cursorily, because his trigger finger knew that if it didn't draw the trigger back pronto, he himself would take a half-ounce chunk of lead through his brisket.

He heard the man grunt beneath the loud belch of Longarm's own rifle, saw him stumble backward. The bushwhacker got his feet beneath him and tried bringing the rifle up once more, and Longarm reluctantly drilled him again.

He'd wanted to take him alive. How else would he find out what in hell had gotten his neck in a hump?

The man twisted around, stumbled forward, dropped his rifle, and fell to his knees, crouching forward.

"Son of a bitch!" he raked out.

Longarm turned and crabbed down to the low side of the roof. He dropped to the ground, ran around to the other side of the coop, and dropped to a knee beside the buckwhacker, just as the man's face smashed against the ground.

"Who are you and why'd you try to beef me, you son of a bitch?" Longarm jerked the man by the collar of his wool coat.

The man only shook his head and sighed. He puffed his cheeks out. He released the air, quivered, and lay still.

Dead.

"Goddamnit." Longarm ran a gloved hand across his mouth in frustration, staring down at the dead man. He frowned at the cheek facing him then used his rifle to shove the man onto his back. He leaned over him and saw the round, fleshy face of Kansas Pete Durant.

"I'll be damned," Longarm said. "Pete, what the hell are you doin' way up here?" The dead man did not answer but merely stared up at the lawman through half-closed lids. He seemed to wear a faint smile, amused by taking his story to the grave.

Longarm didn't wonder why the man would want to kill him. Kansas Pete was a federal criminal, with a hefty price on his head. Maybe that's what explained what he was doing here—avoiding lawmen as well as bounty hunters.

Still, Longarm couldn't help thinking there was another reason why Kansas Pete had tried to trim his wick this night.

Catherine's voice called from behind him, "Custis?"

He turned to see her shadow moving slowly up in back of him, the pistol in her hand winking in the star- and moonlight peeking through the clouds.

"Yeah," he said.

"I figured if there was shooting, you'd be in the middle of it." She stopped a few feet away from him, looked down at the dead man, and then frowned curiously up at Longarm again.

"Catherine Fortescue, meet Kansas Pete Durant."

"Rather ugly," Catherine said, nudging the man's nearest foot with her boot toe. "That why you shot him?"

Longarm stared down at Kansas Pete. "What I wanna know is—why was he gunnin' for me? He couldn't have figured I was gunnin' for him 'cause I wasn't. Hell, I got my hands full with ole Goldie and the wolves and whatnot."

"I prefer to be called Catherine," she said, giving him a devilish glance.

Longarm got serious. "What the hell are you doin'

out here? Wolves on the prowl, and not just the four-legged kind."

She hiked a shoulder. "I heard the shooting, figured you might need a hand. The general has passed out with his head in the lap of Blue Feather—that's his courtesan—and the others are all in their cups, as well."

"You go back inside where it's safe," Longarm said. "I still haven't made it over to the jailhouse yet." He froze, staring at her, a thought dawning on him. "Ah, shit!"

"What?"

Longarm started running through a break between the hardware store and another building left of it. "I got me a feelin' Kansas Pete's part of a bunch here to spring Goldie! You get inside the saloon an' stay there, girl!"

He'd taken two more strides before a wolf snarled behind him, freezing his blood.

Catherine screamed, *"Custis!"*

Chapter 12

"Catherine!" Longarm wheeled and ran back in the direction from which he'd come.

There was another snarl and then the girl screamed once more. A pistol popped. He saw the flashes as he bolted out of the break between the buildings.

Catherine was on the ground near the woodpile, a wolf lying a few feet away from her, flopping around, wounded. Two more milled with their heads down, eyes glowing in the shadows on the woodpile's far side. They shifted their heads toward Longarm, and just as he aimed his Winchester, they turned on a dime and ran off into the darkness.

"Shit!" Catherine sat up and looked at her left arm. "Bastard bit me."

Longarm ran over, drilled another pill through the wounded wolf, killing it, and knelt beside Catherine. "How bad?"

"Not bad."

"Did it draw blood?"

"Well, yeah, it's bleeding." The girl looked at him, her brows coming together. "What—you think I'm going to be a werewolf now?"

Longarm didn't like the way his mind hesitated, the way he forwent answering the question to say, "Best get it wrapped and get you inside." He unknotted his neckerchief, unbuttoned her coat, slid the coat off her shoulder and down her arm.

Blood shone in the light of the moon and stars. Not a lot but enough to give him pause. It had occurred to him that what might have sickened the folks who'd been bit around Crazy Kate was rabies, and that was little comfort.

Quickly, looking around to make sure no more wolves were near, he wrapped the girl's arm then pulled her coat back up onto her shoulder and helped her to her feet. "Get on inside. Take the back stairs and do not—I repeat do not—let anyone know you were bit."

"Don't worry—I don't intend to end up in the jailhouse cellar." Catherine kissed Longarm's cheek as he took her good arm and began leading her back toward the saloon. "Thanks, Custis. And don't worry. I'll be fine. We Fortescues have the fortitude of mustangs."

"The sex drive, too." He turned her loose at the bottom of the stairs and glanced around again, happy not to see any more wolves lurking near. "Go on. Take a hot bath. Douse that wound with plenty of whiskey."

"Will you be up soon?" she asked, raising her brows expectantly.

"You'll be the first to know. Go!"

He waited at the bottom of the stairs, keeping watch with his rifle cocked, until she'd slipped into the saloon's second-story door. That bite preyed on him.

The wolf that had bit her hadn't looked rabid. Still, it preyed on him.

He found himself glancing at the moon kiting high over the town before he lowered his Winchester's hammer to off-cock and strode around the far side of the Carpathian, heading for the jailhouse. Lord only knew what brand of trouble he'd find over there.

The lamp in the jailhouse's front window was still lit.

Approaching cautiously, Longarm studied the front of the place, probing the shadows for more would-be bushwhackers. He studied the window, as well, but spied no movement inside, which may or may not have been a good thing. Vaguely, he wondered if Calvin and Emil had made it back from their chore. How long could it take to run the wolves to the town's edge and dump them, unless they decided to take them farther so the stench of the rotting carcasses wouldn't bother the villagers.

Or maybe the sheriff and his deputy had themselves been harassed by more wolves.

Longarm aimed the Winchester straight out from his right hip as he approached the jailhouse's front door. Quickly, he jerked the door open, aimed the Winchester inside, index finger taut across the trigger. His eyes skidded across the scarred planks, probing the shadows expanding and contracting with the lantern's flickering light.

The cells at the back of the place were in relative darkness, but he could see no one hunkered there or anywhere else, ready to perforate him. Stepping inside, he drew the door closed behind him and walked over to the trapdoor. Goldie's pals could be down in the Wolf Hold, but he didn't hear anything.

Only one way to find out for sure.

He drew the door up and let it slam against the floor. The small, square hole gaped at him. The hole was about as well lit as the marshal's office—he could see the flicker of a lamp's glow.

Dropping to his knees, Longarm lowered his head into the hole and looked around carefully. Nothing but dirt and the earthen bank in which the heavy, wooden, iron-banded doors to the cells were embedded. He could hear a quiet sobbing—the boy who'd been bit by the wolf earlier. Longarm took his rifle in one hand, grabbed the ladder's top rung with the other hand, and dropped straight down into the hole, hitting the dirt floor with a *thud*.

He aimed the rifle out from his hip again, looking around, pleasantly surprised to see that there was no one down here, either. Unless they'd already taken what they'd come for. But Goldie's cell door was closed.

Longarm walked down the narrow corridor, noticing that a ceiling beam lay on the floor to his left, at the base of the hole's left wall. One end was rotted and likely had to have been replaced with the newer looking one running across the ceiling, perpendicular to the cells on Longarm's right. The wall at the end of the narrow corridor was paneled in heavy planks, likely to keep the bank from falling into the hole, as it appeared to have done at one time. An earth tremor, no doubt. Such shifts happened occasionally in the San Juans.

Apparently, the Wolf Hold had been hastily dug, fear having been the primary motivation, and it hadn't been braced as well as it was now.

Sobs emanated from the second door beyond Goldie's, but the brunt of Longarm's attention was on the outlaw's cell. He looked through the small, barred window to see the outlaw sitting on a cot inside, beneath the flaring torch angling out from a wall bracket.

The man was awake. He looked grim, sitting there with a knee up, one arm resting across it, a cigarette smoldering between his fingers. Goldie looked at Longarm and said in a deep, raspy, tired voice, "Would you tell that little peckerwood yonder to shut up? I'm in pain in here, with no fuckin' whiskey to ease it, and I gotta listen to him and his ma?"

"Nice to see ya again, Goldie."

Longarm continued on past the outlaw's cell, stopped in front of the next one, and peered inside. The boy, David, was there, and his mother, a pretty sandy-haired woman in her thirties, sat with her child on the cell's sole cot. The boy lay under a single quilt and what Longarm figured was the woman's ratty coat, jerking as he sobbed, tears running down his pale, red-mottled face. Mrs. Leonard sat as though chilled, staring miserably up through the window at Longarm.

"This is no way to treat a boy," she said, tears oozing from her eyes. "Locking him up when he's injured!"

"I do apologize, ma'am. If I had the key, I'd turn him loose." Longarm paused, and when she turned to smooth the boy's hair back from his forehead with her hand, he added, "You look cold. You oughta have a few more quilts in here."

"Don't do us any favors, mister," the woman said without looking at Longarm, her voice forlorn.

"Yeah, don't do 'em any favors, Longarm." This from Goldie standing in the window of his own cell door, looking out. "Me, though, I could use a woman and a bottle of whiskey. If I'm gonna turn into a werewolf and be fed a silver bullet, I should be allowed that much first."

"Shut up, Goldie."

"Shut up yourself, Lawman!" Goldie yelled as Longarm started toward the ladder.

Longarm glimpsed something from the corner of his eye, and he turned back around and walked down to the end of the corridor. Frowning, he crouched to peer between the boards lining the earthen wall at the end of the hall. He poked his finger between the boards, withdrew the thing that had caught his eye, stared at the tip. Shrugging, he wiped his finger on his pants.

"What you doin' over there, Longarm?" Goldie said. "Lose your way?"

Longarm walked past Goldie's door.

"Hey, bring me a bottle, will ya?" the outlaw shouted.

"If you promise to shut up."

"Oh, I promise, Longarm. Honest!"

When he'd climbed up into the marshal's office, Longarm looked around for some more blankets. He found a couple on the jail cots, but they were so sour with the smell of man sweat and urine that he decided to look elsewhere. Closing the jailhouse door, he headed back across the street to the Carpathian House. He'd just stepped up on the boardwalk when he saw someone moving toward him on his right—a woman in a long fur coat crossing the side street. She had a scarf over her head.

"Don't worry—you won't need that, Marshal Long."

Longarm looked down at the rifle he was aiming at her, and lowered the piece. He recognized the brown eyes inside the red scarf. They belonged to the handsome woman he'd seen in the rear door of the whore-house, who'd come to the aide of the wolf-bit boy and his mother. "You have me at a disadvantage, Miss . . ."

"*Mrs.*," she said, stopping before him, the wind nip-ping at her scarf, blowing the fur coat about her legs. "Mrs. Zeena Radulescu. Was that you making all the gun racket earlier?"

Longarm ignored the question. "You shouldn't be out here."

"I'm probably better equipped to be out here than you are." Zeena pulled a small, pearl-gripped, .36-caliber Remington from a deep pocket of her coat, and let it flash in the moonlight before returning it to her pocket. "Loaded with silver bullets." She glanced at Longarm's Winchester, which he held straight down along his right leg. "Is yours?"

"Nope. I don't believe in all that fairy tale stuff."

"By the time you leave here . . . *if* you leave here . . . I'm betting you will." She turned and opened the saloon door, mentioning over her shoulder, "I came for some booze. The moon and the wolves have me doing a booming business. No one wants to be alone, especially the old prospectors in the less secure shacks down by the creek."

Longarm followed her into the saloon and closed the door. Heads swung toward them, everyone startled by the door opening on this wolf-haunted night. He fol-lowed her through the thick smoke to the bar, and when she'd bought her three bottles of whiskey, Longarm asked the rangy bartender for some blankets for David Leonard and his mother. "Some food would be nice, too," he added.

"How nice of you," Zeena said, her lustrous brown eyes giving him a faintly quizzical appraisal. "A lawman with a heart—imagine." He'd noticed that she spoke with an accent—one that he supposed harkened back to her home country of Romania or Transylvania, or one of those other mysterious Eastern European countries some of the folks around here hailed from.

The barman canted his head toward what was left of the free lunch atop the bar to Longarm's right. "That's all I got," he said. "S'pose you could make 'em a coupla sandwiches. I'll see if I can rustle up some blankets."

When the barman had disappeared through a door flanking the stairs, Longarm walked over and began building a sandwich with ham and cheese and what appeared to be a cold elk roast. There wasn't much of anything left, but it would have to do.

Zeena set her bottles atop the bar then came over, picked up a tin plate, and started building a sandwich. "I'll help you with these," she said. "Does Calvin have coffee over there?"

"None on the stove."

"No, he wouldn't—the cheap bastard." Zeena set a slender slice of elk meat on a slice of bread, covered the meat with another slice of bread, and added a pickled egg to the plate. "I'll fetch some from my place and meet you over there." She set the plate down near the lawman's left elbow, swiping her hands together to dislodge the crumbs.

"What is your place?" Longarm asked, though he thought he knew.

"A whorehouse," she said as she picked up her liquor bottles, her eyes flashing like varnished oak in the sunlight as she regarded him with amusement. "Don't I look like a madam, Marshal Long?"

Longarm glanced at her as he set the food on a single plate to make it easier to carry to the marshal's office with the blankets. "Most of them are old, fat, and ugly," he said, appreciating the woman's beauty despite the crow's-feet around her eyes.

She was likely approaching middle age, but while her body was lush and full, with round womanly hips, she was nothing near fat. She radiated an earthy energy. Her mouth was wide and sensuous, accustomed to smiling, albeit wryly; her long nose bespoke assurance, her eyes faintly jeering in a bawdy sort of way.

Longarm had a feeling she'd be every bit as much a catamount in the mattress sack as Catherine Fortescue.

"And they ain't married," he added, running his eyes back up from her legs to her face.

"I'm a widow." She continued to the door, cradling the bottles in her arms and glancing at him—coquettishly?—over her shoulder. "I'll see you at the marshal's office shortly."

The rangy barman came back with a heavy quilt and a blanket. "This is all I could find," he said, squinting through the smoke of the quirley drooping from between his lips.

"They'll do. Give me a bottle of something cheap, too, will you?"

When he'd paid the man for Goldie's bottle, Longarm wrapped the bottle inside the blankets. He set the plate on top of the bundle, scooped his rifle off the counter, and headed back out into the chilly night.

He paused on the porch and surveyed the shadow-ensconced street. The moon was a couple of hours away from its zenith. It appeared to be getting bigger and brighter.

The wolf's forlorn cry cut through the night once more. Longarm looked above the false-fronted buildings on the opposite side of the street, toward the dark cliffs rising in the north. The convent was up there. It was hard to tell because of the echoes, but he thought the wolf's call was originating up there somewhere.

Crazy Kate? They said she'd been bit by the same wolf that had torn her beau apart.

An uneasy feeling churned in Longarm's belly. Suppressing it, holding the blankets and the plate in his left arm against his chest, clutching the rifle in his right hand, he dropped down off the porch steps and angled across the street to the marshal's office. He had to set his rifle down to open the door with his right hand.

When the door withdrew into the office, two shadowy figures stood before him, about ten feet away. They were dressed in heavy coats, and they were both holding pistols on him.

"Come on in, Mr. Lawdog, suh," said one of them in a thick Southern accent. "We're gonna be needin' a key to get our pal Goldie out of the lockup down below."

Beneath the Southerner's drooping hat brim, he grinned and clicked his pistol hammer back.

Chapter 13

Longarm scowled, silently cursing himself. He should have been more careful. He'd been so preoccupied with the wolf that was continuing to howl once every fifteen or twenty seconds that he'd forgotten about the human wolves out to break Goldie out of the lockup.

"Cannady said get in here, mister!" barked the man to the left of the first man who'd spoken. "My cousin's waitin' down below. We ain't got all night!"

Longarm glanced at his rifle leaning against the jail-house's outer wall and then stepped into the marshal's office. A third man who'd been standing behind the door came up and gave him a hard shove, sending him stumbling into the office, and clamped a hand over one of the sandwiches on the plate atop the blankets.

"We aim to haul our asses out of here while we still can," the man behind him said in a tight voice that was also pitched with a Southern accent. He bit into the sandwich and chewed. He was a short, stocky gent with an eye patch and a ragged beard. Longarm recognized him as the killer known as Henry Paul Winedark.

"You mean before the full moon?" Longarm said, glancing at the trapdoor, which was open. "You're a tad late. Best be careful—Goldie got bit." He gave a wolfish smile, winking. "Might be a werewolf."

Just then, as though to add a chilling theatrical effect to Longarm's words, the wolf loosed its cry from on high. The long, mournful howl swooped gently down over Crazy Kate and sort of ricocheted off the main street before beginning its slow ascent back toward the rocky peaks from which it had come.

The three outlaws stiffened, and each glanced toward the front window or the open door. Winedark tossed the sandwich outside and kicked the door closed, while the second man who'd spoken, Goldie's cousin, whom Longarm recognized as Tater Clark, said, "Key!"

"I don't have it."

"Sure enough you have it." Tater walked toward Longarm. He wore gloves, but the fingers had been cut from the glove on his right hand, making it easier to grasp the long-barreled Colt he now held level with the lawman's belly. He was a pug-faced rapscallion with a thick, red scar running down from beneath his battered Stetson to a tight knot beneath his chin. "Hand it over or I'll drill a forty-five hole through your belly button. Love to, in fact. Get you off our trail once and for all."

Longarm knew they'd clean his clock before they left here no matter what he did. Which meant he had to act fast. His mind raced through his options while he maintained a calm expression, saying, "I'd be obliged if you fellas got Goldie out of my *hair* once and for all.

But it ain't gonna happen, old son. For the last time, I don't have the key."

The first man who'd spoken, Cannady, opened his mouth to speak again but stopped when Goldie yelled from the Wolf Hold, "Bring the fuckin' key, boys. What're you doin' up there? Invitin' ole Longarm to a hoedown?"

Cannady shouted at the hole in the floor, "He says he don't have it."

"*He has it!*" Goldie returned, his voice shrill with impatience. "*Get it from him and let's haul our asses outta this wolf-haunted town!*"

Tater continued toward Longarm, extending his left hand. "Hand over the hogleg, lawdog."

Longarm looked around for a place to set the blankets and the plate on which the remaining sandwich lay. "No, you just hold on to them blankets," Tater said, reaching forward to grab the remaining sandwich. He chomped into it and said around the mouthful of meat and bread, "But I'll lighten your load just a little."

"Quit fuckin' around, Tater," said Cannaday. "Get that key off him."

"I'm waitin' for him to hand over his hogleg."

"Ah, for chrissakes," Cannady said, striding forward and raising his pistol. "Just shoot the son of a bitch. We'll take it off his carcass."

Tater chuckled, spitting out chunks of bread and meat, as he stepped out of Cannady's way. "Here goes, Longarm," Cannady said, smiling grimly, dark eyes flashing devilishly in the flickering lamplight. "End of the trail. I reckon this'll make me right famous, won't it? Hell, I might even get written up in them penny dreadfuls."

Longarm's belly tightened as the man leveled his Remington .44 at the lawman's head, squinting one eye to drill a slug just above the bridge of Longarm's nose. Longarm was a quarter second away from lurching forward to do whatever he could to save his life, when footsteps sounded on the boardwalk fronting the jailhouse. The door behind the three outlaws opened suddenly. Behind Cannady and his cocked Remington, Longarm watched as Zeena Radulescu walked into the jail office with a corked stone jug and two stone mugs in her hands.

All three outlaws, including Cannady, swung their heads toward her suddenly. They swung their guns around, as well, likely expecting Frank Calvin and his giant deputy, Emil.

"Zeena, drop!" the lawman shouted as he let the blankets and plate fall to the floor. At the same time, he bolted forward and wrapped his left arm around Cannady's long, slender neck while chopping his gun arm down with his other hand.

Cannady screamed and triggered his Remington into his right boot. He didn't have time to scream again before Longarm jerked back hard on the man's hand, evoking a sharp *pop!* as Cannady's neck broke like a dry tree branch.

As the other two men swung back toward Longarm, he drew Cannady back against him, using the man for a shield. He grabbed the Remington out of Cannady's suddenly slack fingers and hastily aimed it at Tater Clark, who fired his own pistol at the same time Cannady's roared, the two reports together sounding like an iron rod rapping against an empty tin rain barrel.

Clark's bullet hammered into Cannady, causing the

fast-dying brigand to jerk against Longarm's chest. As Longarm's own slug punched a quarter-sized hole through Tater's right cheek, jerking the bulldog's head back sharply, Winedark loosed an angry holler and fired his own Colt twice.

Both of those rounds also punched the slack-headed Cannady back against Longarm. Longarm fired the Remy once, twice, three times, causing John Paul Winedark to scrunch up his lone eye and bellow miserably while dancing a bizarre two-step around and back out the open door and into the street. Zeena had dropped her coffee jug and mugs and thrown herself to one side, but now she rolled onto a hip and watched as Winedark fell in a pile about six feet away from the jailhouse.

Outside, a horse whinnied.

"What in hell?" Frank Calvin's voice said above the clattering of a wagon approaching the marshal's office.

Longarm flung the dead Cannady aside and knelt down beside Zeena, who was staring at the smoking pistol he still held in his hand. "You're good with that thing."

"Ah, that was nothin'." Longarm clutched her shoulders, raking his eyes across her, looking for bloody wounds, for she might have caught a ricochet. "You all right?"

She nodded.

Outside, the wagon stopped clattering, and Frank Calvin said, "Longarm, that you shootin' my place up?"

"Bustling night, Marshal." Longarm helped Zeena to her feet then picked up her coffee jug and both mugs. "None of 'em broke," he said, handing them to her.

She swept her dark brown hair from her eyes and drew a ragged breath. "Miracle of miracles."

Longarm went outside to where Calvin and Emil were climbing down from the wagon they'd parked parallel to the hitch rack, a few feet from where Winedark lay facedown in the hard-packed street, being dusted with the fine snow that was falling from a passing cloud, though the moon still shone. The killer had rolled onto his side and was fishing his second pistol out of its holster, breathing hard and cursing.

Longarm shot him through the head. He supposed he could have snatched the gun out of the outlaw's hand before the killer leveled it on him, but John Paul Winedark was going to die anyway. Why put him and Longarm through the trouble of getting him tended? The federal had heard enough of Goldie's caterwauling.

Calvin and Emil, who towered over the silver-mustached town marshal, stood looking down at the dead brigand. Calvin looked at Longarm, frowning, the snow slanting in beneath his black hat brim and catching in his grizzled brows.

"Goldie's pards," Longarm said.

"Wolf bait now," said Calvin.

Longarm looked at him and his giant deputy. "Where you two been?"

"We took the wolves to a ravine northeast of town, decided to keep watch over 'em in case their pards came to inspect. Wolves will do that, sort of hang around the fallen amongst 'em. Figured we'd take a few down, cull the herd."

"Did any show?"

Calvin shook his head and glanced at Emil. "Load up Longarm's dead. We'll house 'em in the stable till tomorrow then take 'em out to where we hauled the wolves. No point in hirin' the undertaker to bury 'em."

As Emil brushed past Longarm to pick up Winedark, the federal lawman regarded the local incredulously. "Won't that just attract more wolves?"

Calvin had started into the marshal's office. "You wanna bury 'em, Marshal Long, then you bury 'em. Personally, I don't think it's such a good idea to remain outside long enough to dig a grave and sing a prayer over known killers." The town marshal glanced around. "Any other trouble this evenin'?"

"Oh, hell yeah," Longarm said. "Busy damn night. Not long after you and Emil left, an old friend by the name of Kansas Pete Durant tried to bore me a third eye. One I couldn't see out of even with glasses."

"Damn, Longarm," Calvin said as Emil, having tossed Winedark into the back of the wagon like so much trash, ducked into the marshal's office to retrieve the other bodies. "You sure do attract trouble. Honestly, I wish you'd leave."

"I'd love to oblige you."

"Any idea when that could happen?"

"Possibly tomorrow, wolves permitting." Longarm was reluctant to leave Catherine and her hunting party, as something told him they might need help getting out of here. But he had a job to do, and that didn't include acting as caretaker of a passel of drunken mucky-mucks.

"Takin' your prisoner?"

"Of course."

Calvin stepped to one side as Emil ducked through the door with Cannady draped over one shoulder and tossed the neck-broke outlaw into the wagon with Winedark. "Might have to take him in chains." The local lawman slanted an eye at the moon angling westward. "He just might turn."

"Yeah, yeah," Longarm said, his skeptical grumbling belying his apprehension. He canted his head at the marshal's office. "Mrs. Radulescu's inside. She has coffee for Mrs. Leonard. I brought extra blankets over from the saloon."

"Ain't that sweet of both of you." Calvin snorted, habitually belligerent, and walked inside the jailhouse. "Good Lord," he raked out above the clomping of his boots. "Smells like the devil's blood in here!"

Chapter 14

"Why do you have so damn many wolves around here, Calvin?" Longarm asked later, after the marshal had gone down and opened David Leonard's cell door for Zeena. "Personally, I've rarely seen such an infestation. Those I did see were out on the prairie, when there was a white-tail explosion. Or around hide-hunting camps where there was plenty of fresh meat and hides lyin' around."

Longarm leaned back in his chair and scratched a lucifer to light on his thumbnail. Touching the flame to the end of a fresh, three-for-a-nickel cheroot and puffing smoke, he added, "I've seen a coupla mining camps stalked by wolves, when the miners had hunted most of the game out of the area and they weren't buryin' their trash proper, to keep the smell down, but that was only a small pack. Five, maybe six wolves. Seems to me you must have several packs convergin' here on Crazy Kate."

He waved the match out. Smoke wafted papery

blue in the light of the lantern flickering atop Calvin's desk.

The marshal sat in his swivel chair fronting the desk. His hat was off, his silver hair matted down close to his head. He sat back in the chair, his thick, red-brown hands, the nails black with caked grime, laced over his flat belly clad in a blue plaid shirt over a red longhandle shirt. He wore a blue neckerchief knotted to one side.

Emil had driven off in the wagon loaded with dead men. Calvin appeared to study the floor thoughtfully, pondering the federal lawman's question. Finally, he looked up at Longarm faintly bleary-eyed, weary. "You see, I was as puzzled as you were, once upon a time. 'Cause I ain't from here. I'm from off a ranch over on the west side of the Sangre de Cristo range. Owned the place . . . until I was rooted out by bigger cattlemen. My wife was dead, so I had nothin' much to do or live for till I wandered through Crazy Kate and saw they needed a town marshal.

"That was six years ago," Calvin continued, staring out the window above his desk. "I been here since. And I can tell you that at least during that six years, this country has been plagued by wolves. Maybe not as many as now, but wolves always have caused trouble hereabouts. All through the San Juans, but around Crazy Kate especially. At first, I figured it was because the valley's so deep and long and there happens to be several packs callin' it their territory, and during the long winters these packs got used to preyin' on men and livestock. They're a sneaky bunch, so they've avoided hunters."

Calvin continued to stare out the window, beyond which the moon hung like a giant, glowing globe. He'd started a fire in his bullet-shaped stove, and the stove's iron ticked as it heated, the flames sounding like snakes slithering around in a croaker sack.

Longarm drew deep on his cigar and blew a long plume toward the empty cells crouched in the shadows at the back of the jailhouse. "You said you *figured* that was happening. Now you're dead certain these ain't just your regular brand of wolves runnin' around."

He looked at the town marshal, who turned his head slightly toward him. A fire sparked in his eyes, and he drew a hard breath as he said, "This town is cursed, Longarm. I'm tellin' you, it's cursed. The folks who first settled here brought said curse with 'em from Eastern Europe."

He shook his head slowly, keeping his red-rimmed eyes pinned on the federal lawman. "I know you won't believe that, so I don't know why we're havin' this conversation. Hell, talk to Zeena about it. Mrs. Radulescu. She knows!"

"Oh, I heard what she has to say about it."

Frustrated, Calvin shook his head.

Longarm frowned at the man, genuinely puzzled. "Why in the hell are you hangin' around here, if you're so scared?"

"Here's why." Calvin stared even harder, more penetratingly, at Longarm. "Because once you're here for a while, you become cursed, as well. If you leave here, you'll just take it with you. That's why you best get the hell out of here, Mr. Federal Lawdog. Before the curse gets inside of you, too. And believe me, it's a curse you don't never wanna be cursed with! Once you're cursed, it'll follow you wherever you go!"

The ladder beneath the hole in the floor creaked.

Longarm saw the top of Zeena Radulescu's head, and he got up quickly and walked over to give her a hand up the ladder. She brushed dust from her coat and glanced between Longarm and the local lawman, then arched her brows. "Sounded like a very serious conversation, gentlemen."

"I guess you could say that," Calvin said. "How's the boy?"

"None the better for being down in that hole, Frank. Isn't there some other way? I mean, even if he changes, he—"

"You know the rules, Zeena," the lawman said. "Anyone bit around the time of the full moon is locked in the Wolf Hold until we know for sure that he . . . or she, for that matter . . . is not one o' *them* out there." He pointed at the moonlit window over his desk.

Zeena sighed and glanced at Longarm. "He's a stubborn man, our marshal."

"That he is."

"Oh, well. He should be out of there in a few hours. He's a tough young man. He'll make it."

"Unless he turns," Longarm said, probingly, giving a grim, lopsided smile.

"Yes," Zeena said. "Unless he turns."

"And then he gets a silver bullet." Longarm glanced at Calvin, who merely sat in his chair, boots together on the floor, knees spread, hands still entwined on his belly. Calvin didn't nod. His resolute eyes were answer enough.

Zeena brushed a hand across Longarm's blood-stained buckskin mackinaw, something to remember Cannady by. "I can get that blood out, if you like. Follow me over to the Black Wolf?"

"The Black Wolf?"

"That's my place of business, Marshal Long. Zeena's Black Wolf House of a Thousand Delights. My sign is tastefully small. You might have missed it."

"Go on over," Calvin said. "You'll like it over there, Longarm. Zeena's fixed the place up nice, made it a special haven for men on nights like this one here. A wolf-on-the-prowl kinda night." He lifted one cheek in a devilish half smile. "Less you got somethin' else goin' on over at the Carpathian?"

Longarm glanced at Zeena, who gave him a similarly foxy smile. Obviously, she'd seen Catherine Fortescue and had rightfully ascertained Longarm's relationship with the girl.

He thought he should head over there and see how Catherine was doing, since she'd been wolf-bit, but she was likely asleep. He'd wait and check on her later. There was still plenty of night to get through, and he might as well get his coat washed out. It was the only one he had, and it wouldn't be fitting for him to go around with it bloodstained.

"I'd be obliged for your assistance, Mrs. Radulescu," he said with a courtly nod of his head, and went over to retrieve his Winchester from where he'd leaned it against the wall by Calvin's desk. He racked a fresh round in the chamber, lowered the piece, and off-cocked the hammer. He looked at Calvin, read the man's mind, and said, "It ain't silver, but I reckon it'll have to do."

He turned to Zeena and hooked his arm. "Shall we, Mrs. Radulescu?"

"We shall, Marshal," the woman said, taking his arm and allowing him to lead her out of the marshal's office.

"You two kids have a good time," Calvin said behind them, as Longarm closed the door.

He and the woman started along the street toward Zeena's Black Wolf House of a Thousand Delights. They were halfway between the jailhouse and the sporting parlor, which was just down from and on the same side of the street as the Carpathian, when the wolf called from the direction of the lofty convent. Zeena gasped slightly and stopped for a moment, swinging her head to the north.

"Crazy Kate, you think?" Longarm asked.

"Think?" Zeena said. "Marshal Long, I know."

Longarm frowned. "You really think a woman, even a crazy woman, could kick up such a racket? And sound that much like a wolf?"

Zeena regarded him as though he were a particularly thickheaded schoolboy. "Yes, I do."

"Have you seen her?"

"No. I don't think anyone's seen her since they took her up to the convent. Only the nuns, and they don't grant access to anyone not their own. But rumors come from there, mostly about Katarina."

They continued walking along the south side of the street, heading toward the dimly lit whorehouse that was a relatively unadorned three-story building with a balcony on each of the two upper stories. The blazing moonlight held it in dark silhouette.

"Rumors about how she becomes a werewolf during each full moon?" Longarm asked her as they mounted the parlor's narrow front porch. There was a small shingle attached to the front wall, to the right of the house's door, that had a wolf's head burned into it along with the name: ZEENA'S BLACK WOLF HOUSE OF A THOUSAND DELIGHTS.

"That's right. I can tell you it frightens the nuns terribly, but they keep her locked in a tower room away from the main part of the convent. She does no harm when she turns, they say, though several nuns haven't been able to endure the strain of it, and ran away."

Longarm followed Zeena through the front door and into a red-carpeted lobby. Oil lamps burned in wall brackets, illuminating several paintings—secured to the walls—of wolves. The frames and the faded paintings themselves looked old, probably having come from the Old Country. Some depicted the wolves dancing on their hind legs with children.

There was also a sculpture of a black wolf's head serving as the newel post for the stairs that rose at the hall's rear, beyond several closed doors. There was a small, horseshoe-shaped, hotel-like desk in front of the stairway. No one sat behind it. Longarm figured that was probably Zeena's customary spot.

The place was eerily quiet except for the very faint singing of what sounded like a very young girl, to the delicate patter of a piano, somewhere in the building's upper reaches. The air was rife with the smell of candles, incense, and the slightly spicy-musky odor of what could only be opium.

No wonder everyone was so quiet, Longarm thought. They were either singing or hopped out on the midnight oil.

Zeena turned to Longarm. "Take your coat off. I have a Chinese gentleman who can get that blood out without a trace. He uses a combination of wax, lard, and a few other things I don't even know the names of."

Longarm shrugged out of the coat. She took it and

disappeared down the hall beyond the stairs before returning a moment later, turning to the stairs, and placing one foot on the bottom step.

She looked back at him obliquely. "Might as well join me for a drink while Li Yu works on the blood. I have to tell you, though, Marshal, that no other man has ever visited my room. I am the madam here, which means I have a certain decorum to maintain. My clothes never leave my body during working hours."

"I'll behave if you will." Longarm grinned and doffed his hat. "And I reckon since I'm bein' bestowed such an honor and privilege, you might as well call me Longarm."

Fifteen minutes later, they'd had a drink in her large room adorned in the same wolf motif as that in the first-story hall, with a fire crackling in a stout hearth, and they smiled at each other from their brocade-upholstered chairs positioned on opposite sides of a round wooden table clothed in silk.

Longarm tossed the last of his brandy back, stood, and began to get undressed.

She stood, as well, and began doing same, her cheeks flushed, seeming a little breathless. Longarm didn't doubt she hadn't had her ashes hauled in a while. She and he both knew it was time. That's why they hadn't said one word to each other during the fifteen minutes they'd sipped their brandy and stared into the fire, enjoying the sensuous heat radiating from the fire like a soft, warm hand.

"What about the girl?"

"What girl?"

Zeena laughed wryly. "That's why I haven't done anything like this since my husband passed four years ago. Out of sight, out of mind. That's the way it is for you, isn't it?"

"I reckon it is if we haven't made any promises." Zeena's breasts were heavy but firm, her body pale and fine. It wasn't a taut young body, but a full, mature one with some extra flesh on it that owned its own, earthy allure.

Longarm hung his cartridge belt and pistol on a bedpost. "You lure me over here for a tongue-lashing?"

"I lured you over here because you're damn handsome. Big and manly. Any woman would like to be held by you. I suppose it harkens back to when we were all living in caves and we women were driven to the best of men for safety, and to father the stoutest offspring. I don't know."

Zeena laughed and sat on the edge of the bed naked, wearing only a gold neck chain with a small wolf figurine carved from obsidian dangling from it between her breasts. "Maybe it's because you're just passing through and I'll never see you again after tonight."

Her eyes widened as he tossed away his balbriggan bottoms and stood before her naked. "Oh," she said, huskily, her voice catching a little. She laughed. "Oh, yes, that will do nicely."

She dropped to her knees before him and ran her admiring eyes up and down the throbbing length of his cock, caressing it tenderly with her fingertips. Longarm could feel her hot breath on him.

"Oh, yes," she breathed. "This will do just fine."

She nuzzled his scrotum and then slid her tongue up the underside of his cock so slowly that he thought he was going to grind his toes right through the thick, plush carpet beneath his feet. Desire jetted in him. He

squeezed his eyes closed. Her tongue slid up to the end
of his cock, and then the heat and wetness of her mouth
closed over it and slid slowly, slowly down, taking
nearly all of him.

Longarm heard himself groan.

When she'd brought him to the edge of the cliff, he
stepped back away from her and sucked a long, calm-
ing breath. She looked up at him, kneading his taut
belly with her hands.

"I'll finish you if you want, Longarm."

"That'd be right selfish of me, wouldn't it?" he
croaked. "Since you said you haven't had it in a while."

"My," she said, looking up at him from beneath his
hard cock, touching the tip of her tongue teasingly to
the end of it. "Maybe I misjudged you."

She rose from the floor, turned the bedcovers back,
and climbed in. Longarm climbed in after her. She
fluffed the pillow and lay her head down on top of it,
staring up at him with those beguiling brown eyes that
were turned up ever-so-slightly at the corners, giving
them a Slavic slant. They were framed by her long, dark
brown hair that curled down over her shoulders to
caress the sides of her heavy, sloping breasts, the nipples of each tilted to the side and fully distended.

As he mounted her, he could feel the wetness of her
need. She lifted her head and looked down at his cock,
spreading her legs, taking his iron-hard dong in both
of her hands, and holding it tightly against her snatch.

He held himself suspended on his arms and the tips
of his toes while she closed her eyes and pleasured herself very slowly with the head of his cock, running it
up and down the warm, soft entrance to her woman-
hood. Her breasts rose and fell sharply, and he leaned

his head down to lick and nuzzle them, to suck each nipple in turn.

"Oh," she said. "Oh . . . oh, Christ . . . oh . . . oh . . . !"

Then she opened her eyes, smiled up at him, showing nearly all of her pearl-white teeth, and slipped his massively swollen head inside her. She wrapped her hands around his ass and drew him into her. He felt his cock, like a warm, sparking nerve, sliding into her—deep down and then up inside her womb, toward her belly, until it wouldn't go any farther.

He slid back out, and she sighed.

He slid back in, and she groaned.

He tried to slide back out again, but she held him there, and she herself tightened—every inch of her—tipping her head far back on the pillow until the cords stood out in her neck.

He felt her pussy quivering and oozing as she came, drawing her knees up hard against him. When she opened her eyes, she reached up and placed her hands on the sides of his face, holding his head as he began to hammer against her, smiling at him ethereally until he, too, had taken himself over the edge and felt the hot, relieving burst of release.

He squeezed his eyes closed and held himself hard against her as the final spasms rippled through him.

He felt something small and cold press against his chest. Opening his eyes, he looked down to see that she was holding her pearl-gripped pocket pistol against his sternum. She clicked the hammer back. Her brown eyes owned a sad cast as she said, "I'm sorry to have to end such a wonderful night this way, Custis."

Chapter 15

"No need to apologize," Longarm said, keeping his still-hard cock deep inside her. "I took the bullets out when you were building a fire earlier."

Zeena pulled the Remington's trigger. The hammer dropped with a click. Her mouth opened slightly in shock. "How . . . did . . . ?"

"While I don't believe in beatin' around the bush myself, you just seemed to come on a little too strong for someone I take to be the naturally reserved sort."

She frowned angrily and pulled the pistol's trigger again, again, and again, until the hammer had clicked five more times. Longarm smiled grimly down at her, took the popper out of her hands, and pulled out of her. She threw her head back against the pillow with an enraged grunt.

Longarm dropped his feet to the floor and glanced over his shoulder at her. "Why?"

She lay naked on top of the bed, staring at the ceiling

in defeat. Still, she summoned some steel into her voice
as she said, "Go to hell."

"Better tell me or I'll haul your ass in on federal
charges. That's what attempting to drill a pill through
a deputy U.S. marshal's heart will get you." Longarm
felt his own anger rise, as it did when folks tried to kill
him. Especially those who had just fucked him. The
two acts did not sit well so close together.

"Come on. Spill it. Who put you up to this? Goldie's
friends? Calvin? Who?"

She lifted her head. "Calvin? Why would he want
you dead?"

"Him and Goldie are about the only two folks I know
in town, and Calvin's made no bones about wanting me
to get my ass out of here sooner rather than later."

Zeena rested her head back against her pillow once
more. She sighed at length and turned her mouth corners down as she continued to stare at the ceiling. "No,
it wasn't Calvin. It was the man you shot earlier. It was
for him."

Longarm scowled, knitting his brows together and
carving a plethora of deeply skeptical lines across his
forehead. "*Kansas Pete Durant?*"

She returned an indignant glare. "I loved him, all
right?"

"You and *Pete Durant*?"

"I just told you I loved him, didn't I?"

"That stuck way up high in my craw, I'm afraid,
Zeena. I just can't see a straight-backed, good-lookin'
woman like yourself—a woman with her own business,
no less—hitchin' her star to the likes of that worthless
bushwhacker!"

"He wasn't worthless anymore," she said, scooting

up to sit against the bed's brass headboard and drawing the quilts and blankets up to cover her breasts. "He'd come up here to hide out about a year ago. He came to work for me, doin' odd jobs about the place, and . . . well . . . he changed." She lowered her voice, made it sound sincerely intimate. "We fell in love. When he saw you, he figured you were here to haul him back to Denver. I tried to get him to forget it, but Pete was one hardheaded man. He said he wouldn't let you take him in. Not alive, anyway. We'd built too much together."

Longarm just stared at her, unable to imagine her and Kansas Pete Durant together. It would be like trying envision a pretty schoolmarm screwing the town drunk. But he had to admit he'd seen it before—two disparate people somehow throwing in together, to the total shock and surprise of everyone who knew them.

He shook his head as he continued to think it through. Behind him, Zeena sobbed quietly. "He was good and gentle. Of course, you wouldn't believe it, but he was as good a man as I'd ever known. He was kind to me. Eventually, we were going to run off to Mexico together."

Her voice turned hard with acrimony. "And you took him away from me, you bastard! What does that leave me?" She sobbed, sniffed. "It leaves me nearing middle age up here in this wolf-haunted village—*alone!* Do you know what it's like for an aging woman *alone*?"

Longarm regarded her with less heat as she sat there, arms crossed on her chest, head down, sobbing. He sighed, heaved himself to his feet, and walked over to the washstand. He set the pistol on the stand, poured water from a pitcher into the basin, and began scrubbing his privates.

"Well, I'll be damned" was all he said.

It was the only thing either of them said. When he finished washing, he dressed, hearing the wolf howling from the northern ridge again. He donned his hat, noted a gathering chill in the room, and added a couple of chunks of split cedar to the stove from the wood box, closing the door afterward with a shrill squawk of the iron handle. He glanced at her once more, staring into empty space through a tangle of hair over her eyes. Then he grabbed his rifle, turned to the door, and stepped into the hall.

He stood there for nearly a minute, staring at the carpet. He couldn't quite wrap his mind around Zeena and Kansas Pete, but there were some things—especially regarding the relations of some men and some women—that just didn't figure. Love was one of them. Damn, she had him feeling bad about killing that no-good killer and general hard case Kansas Pete Durant.

Imagine that.

As he walked along the narrow hall, hearing only a few hushed voices behind the closed doors on either side of him and smelling liquor and the cloying midnight oil, he checked his old turnip watch. Damn near eleven o'clock.

One of those apprehensive twinges he'd been getting of late raked across his spine. It was sort of like being anxious about an upcoming appointment. He gave an amused snort, but again he noted a lack of real amusement in the snort; it expressed only his wanting to feel amused.

He felt genuine trepidation about midnight.

What did he think? he wondered as he headed on

down the stairs, replacing the pocket watch and plucking a cheroot from his shirt pocket. Did he think ole
Goldie and the little boy, David Leonard, were going
to turn into werewolves and run in a bloody killing
frenzy with all the other wolves of Crazy Kate, literally
painting the town red?

He stood out on the Black Wolf's front porch, looking around carefully to make sure he was alone out
there in the chilly darkness, and then he stared up at
the moon. It was about a half hour away from its zenith.
He could see the little pocks and fissures on the lunar
landscape. The sunlight reflecting off it almost seemed
to pulsate, white as a giant pearl.

Again, the wolf on the mountain howled. The call
was as long and mournful and menacing as before. The
echo took a long time to die. When it did, the howl came
again, just like before.

Longarm felt himself shudder and then stepped off
the porch and walked west along the street to the Carpathian, which was still as lit up as it had been several
hours earlier. If anything, it was even busier than before,
as though everyone was celebrating some religious
holiday, though in reality they knew they were all merely
trying to distract themselves from the moon rising ever
higher above the Carpathian's shake-shingled roof.

The general and his hunting party were still there,
at the same table as before. The general had gotten his
second wind, and one of the pudgy local whores was
teaching him how to dance what appeared to be a tra-
ditional dance of the Old Country while a good dozen
other men sat or stood around, stomping their feet and
clapping.

Longarm wended his way through the crowd. He

was tired down deep in his bones, and he only wanted to check on Catherine and find a place to throw down for some sleep. If he could, that was. With the full moon on the rise.

In the second-floor hall, he stopped in front of her door. He turned the knob, expecting the door to be locked, but to his surprise, the latch clicked. He pushed the door open to find a lamp burning dully on the dresser. Catherine lay curled on her side beneath the covers, hair splayed out across her pillow.

Longarm closed the door, leaned his rifle against the dresser, walked over to the bed, and sat on the edge of it. He drew the covers down very gently, so as not to wake her, and exposed her right arm. She'd placed a white bandage over it. The bandage was wet—he could smell the whiskey she'd soaked it with—and slightly blood-spotted. Nothing too severe, though the beast had certainly drawn blood. But she'd live.

As long as she didn't turn into a werewolf in a half hour.

She gasped and snapped her eyes open with a start. "Oh!" she said, settling her head back onto the pillow and smiling. "It's you. Where've you been, Custis?"

"Uh . . . followin' up on a hunch."

"About the man who tried to shoot you?"

"Yeah. How you feelin'?"

"Just fine. I swilled whiskey to kill the pain." Catherine flung the covers back groggily, revealing her long, bare legs beneath a chemise so thin he could see everything under it. "Get undressed and crawl in here, you."

For the first time in his life, Longarm's dong actually sagged down between his thighs at the thought of another mattress dance. That would be how many tussels in one day? He'd lost count.

"I figured I'd go out and keep an eye on things," he lied, intending to hole up for a couple of hours in the livery barn with his horse, where he could probably get a lot more rest than he could here. Even if she didn't want to rassle again, sleeping beside a beautiful woman could be enervating as opposed to restful.

"I won't hear of it," she said. "Even a federal lawman needs his sleep. Get those duds off that big, brawny carcass of yours, and crawl in here and keep me warm."

So that's what he did. It turned out she even let him sleep, as she slept herself with the help of the whiskey. Only, he wasn't sure how much time had passed before she rose from the covers, flung her chemise aside, and rolled on top of him, sitting up and tenting the bedcovers with her body.

She placed his hands on her breasts and threw her head back, flinging her thick hair behind her shoulders. While he kneaded her lovely bosoms, she rubbed her silky snatch around on his cock. He didn't think he had any more lead in the old pistol, but he'd be damned if, after a few minutes of her moist snatch manipulating him, he didn't look down and see that raging hard-on standing at full mast in front of her belly.

She scuttled down his legs a ways, lowered her head, and licked him until he was even harder. She dropped her mouth down over his cock's head, and then she dropped it still farther along the shaft, until he felt her throat pressed up hard against him and heard the liquid sounds of her sucking, the sultry, beguiling sounds of her groaning in pleasure.

When she lifted her head, it was no longer Catherine's head but a wolf's head nearly as large as a cow's. The yellow eyes glowed in the midnight-black sockets. Somehow, they remained Catherine's eyes, only instead of hazel they were yellow. The beasts's hackles rose, shrouding the head in spiky fur, and the upper lips lifted to reveal two-inch-long, ivory-white, razor-edged fangs.

Catherine threw her wolf's head far back on her shoulders, loosed a long, shrill howl, then pointed her long, thick nose toward Longarm once more, growling and snarling savagely.

Longarm loosed a howl of his own as she thrust her teeth toward his throat.

Chapter 16

"Custis!" the wolf screamed.

Longarm stared at the wolf's eyes. They were hazel now. And the wolf's head around them was suddenly Catherine Fortescue's head.

Her very beautiful, human head.

She was staring at him, her eyes bright with terror, sort of leaning back away from him. Longarm realized then why she was the one looking fearful now, for he was staring over the cocked hammer of his .44, which was aimed at the girl's beautiful, human—yes, *human*—head.

He lowered his eyes past her gold necklace to the red-plaid wool shirt she wore beneath her open fur coat. Her mussed, honey-blond hair glistened in the glow of the lamp that had been turned up on the dresser.

His heart hammering painfully against his breast-bone, Longarm looked around for the wolf. No sign of it.

"Custis," she said, loosing a long, relieved breath as

he lowered the Colt, "you were dreaming, honey. Just dreaming."

"Holy shit."

"What . . . were you dreaming?" she asked, the color beginning to return to her cheeks.

Slow to shake the nightmare, still half-believing she was about to tear out his throat, he looked at her arm clad in fur and wool. "How's your arm?"

"Hurts a little," she said, staring at him skeptically. "But it's better." She leaned forward and placed a desperate hand on his shoulder. "Custis, you have to help me. My father . . . his men . . . they've gone out hunting."

He sat up in bed, looking around. The window was dark; it was still night. How long had he been sleeping? "What time is it?"

"Half past midnight."

He swung his feet to the floor, sitting up, blinking groggily, still trying to clear the cobwebs and the image of the yellow-eyed black wolf from his retinas. He looked at her, her words just then penetrating the thick skin of his consciousness. "Did you say . . . ?"

"They went out hunting, Custis. My father and his men." She spoke slowly, as though to a thick child. "They made a bet with a couple of the local men. A thousand-dollar bet that they couldn't kill a wolf and bring it back to the Carpathian."

"What the hell are you sayin', Catherine? Why the hell couldn't they kill a wolf?"

"The local men say that during a full moon, the only thing that will kill the wolves is silver bullets. Father and his men have foolishly, drunkenly taken them up on the challenge, and they've headed out to hunt the wolves with regular bullets and bring at least *one* back to the saloon, though Father boasted that they'd *each* get one!"

"Well, that's just plain reckless," Longarm said, clearer now, rising and looking for his clothes. "Who knows how many wolves are out there? And, hell, who knows if the locals are right or not?"

Catherine remained sitting on the edge of the bed, staring up at him incredulously. "What are you saying? You think they're really *werewolves*?"

"I'm sayin' that if I head out there after wolves tonight, I'd copper my bets and at least use silver bullets." Longarm snorted and shook his head as he shoved one foot into his balbriggan bottoms. "Can't believe I just said that, but there it is. Shit, I'm as crazy as Calvin."

"Will you help me find those idiots and bring them back? I didn't know what they'd done until I went down to the saloon just a few minutes ago, and the local men told me. Despite the moon, it's damn scary out there. I didn't want to go out there alone." Catherine shuddered, hugged herself. "That one wolf keeps howling and howling."

Longarm paused, listening. Sure enough, the wolf was still howling. He wondered if it had been howling steadily since the last time he'd noticed it.

"No, you'd best not go out there alone. In fact, you'd best not go out there at all." Longarm reached for his gun rig, strapped it around his waist. "I'll go find'em and bring 'em back before they're wolf bait." If it isn't too late, the fools, he added to himself.

"I'm going with you!" she insisted as he grabbed his Winchester and headed out of her room, Catherine on his heels.

The full-moon celebration had died down only slightly in the main drinking hall. The place was so smoky that it was like wading through a field after a pitched battle involving a thousand cannons. A couple of the local men, in beards, suspenders, billed watch caps, and with faces wizened from years of the high-country weather, danced together while the others conversed and drank. The whores were still making the rounds, though they looked tired and drawn. One was leading a stocky gent up the stairs as Longarm and Catherine made their ways along the bar to the front door.

Longarm could tell who'd challenged the general and the general's friends to the wolf hunt by the self-satisfied, faintly jeering expressions on a local man's face. Likely one of the original settlers, he had a long, hawk-nosed face with a dark mole on his cheek and slick black hair.

Longarm had seen him before, and because of the man's proud businessman's air, the lawman had assumed that he owned at least a couple of successful enterprises here in Crazy Kate. He was sitting with three others at a table near the ticking potbelly stove. He and his assocaties, all clad in suits and fur hats, were smoking pipes and sitting back in their chairs, waiting to see if any of the arrogant strangers survived the wolf hunt. The bowl of the pipe the challenger was smoking was a carving of a wolf's head.

Outside, the wolf from the north mountain gave its haunting cry as Catherine closed the saloon door behind her and Longarm. Their breath puffed in the chill air. The moon had reached its zenith and was beginning its long, slow fall to the west. It was nearly as light as day out here, though the shadows around buildings and objects were heavy, inky, and menacing with all that they might conceal.

The moonlight made the street look like a river angling between silhouetted ridges. On it, nothing moved. With his eyes Longarm probed the shadows beneath stoops and in alley mouths, and saw no sign of the wolves. He looked at the jailhouse. The lamp in its window had finally gone out.

"Any idea which way they headed?" Longarm asked Catherine.

"No. I came out and called for them a few minutes ago, but I got no reply. They must be a ways away."

Longarm dropped down off the porch steps, squeezing the Winchester in his gloved hands. Part of him wished he had silver bullets for the long gun; another part of him scoffed at the notion.

"You stay close," he said, as he moved out into the street, probing every shadow with his eyes, pricking his ears, trying to get some sense of which direction the general and his moneyed friends had headed.

Between the long, echoing calls of the wolf on the north mountain, a sound came from the northwest. Hard to tell what it was. An echoing snarl? What sounded like a man's yell followed.

Catherine gasped.

"That must be them. Damn Father, the drunken idiot!"

"He do this sort of thing often?" Longarm asked, keeping his voice low as he began walking west along the street.

"You mean does he get drunk with his friends and accept crazy challenges? Yes." Catherine was speaking

just above a whisper, clinging to Longarm's elbow.
"Never anything this crazy, though. I'd thought his trying to lasso a grizzly a couple of months ago was as bad
as it would ever get."

"He must be damn bored."

"I regret that I ever encouraged him to retire," Catherine said.

Longarm continued walking along the street. The
sounds—whatever they were, a commotion of some
kind—continued to rise from what seemed to be the
northwest.

Longarm headed that way, swerving to the right
of the main street, traversing a break between buildings, and then curving westward among cabins, stock
pens, and privies. Most of the cabins he passed were
dark. Longarm assumed that everyone who lived out
here was either in the Carpathian Saloon or in Zeena's
Black Wolf House of a Thousand Delights, or one of
the other smaller watering holes now providing sanctuary from the wild beasts preying on the town.

That was where Longarm should be. Catherine, too.
If her old man wanted to kill himself, let him have it.
No better way to do it than to be out here hunting wolves
in the dark, even if the moon was full. Or, maybe, *especially* if the moon was full . . .

"What an awful smell," Catherine said when they'd
stolen slowly along the edge of the town, between Crazy
Kate and the northern ridge, for about fifteen
minutes.

Longarm had smelled it, too. On his right a large
barn loomed. On his left was a cabin with a caved-in
roof. They'd strayed onto an old farmstead, maybe
home to one of the original settlers. The town had

spread out just south of it. There was no sign that anyone still lived here. The thick, sickly sweet fetor of
putrefying flesh wafted from the direction of the barn.

Suspicion raked at Longarm as he stared at the barn,
frowning.

"Come on," he told Catherine. "I'm gonna check it
out."

As he walked toward the big building hulking before
him, she followed, both of them stepping lightly, he
with his rifle up and ready, she extending her revolver.
They pivoted on their hips and turned their heads back
and forth slowly, looking around. The sounds they'd
been following had died.

The fetor grew stronger with each step Longarm
took toward the barn. The structure's large front doors
were gone, the opening forming a black rectangle
against the moon-silvered front wall. The light pene-
trated only a few feet, laying down a silver prism. By
the time he reached the barn's opening, his eyes were
watering from the stench of decay. Catherine held her
arm over her nose and mouth.

Longarm peered inside but couldn't see anything; in
contrast to the moonlight, the barn's bowels were nearly
as dark as the bottom of a well. Not hearing anything
moving around inside, or seeing any yellow eyes glowing at him, he lit a lucifer and held it up as he walked
into the darkness beyond the door.

The flickering match light revealed a lamp hanging
from a stout post on his right. He lit the lamp and held
it high, walking around, wincing against the horrible,
nearly overpowering smell, breathing through his
mouth to keep from retching.

The sphere of flickering lamplight revealed several

ropes dangling from high rafters. Some of these ropes
held what were obviously the remains of deer or elk,
judging by the sizes of the remaining bones and the
heads that were still suspended in loops a good eight
or ten feet above the barn floor.

Very little meat, hide, or fur remained on the bones.
In fact, some of the ropes held nothing at all, but that
they had once suspended dead animals above the floor
was obvious by the dried red blood that clung to the
hemp.

Lowering the lamp and continuing to move around
the barn, Longarm saw that the floor was thickly car-
peted in more dried blood that crunched when he
walked on it. The floor was strewn with white bones of
all shapes and sizes; they'd been stripped clean, scoured
by feral teeth that had first ripped chunks of the bodies
down from the ropes.

Despite the grisliness of the discovery and the rancid
smell that caused tears to ooze out of his eyes and drib-
ble down his cheeks, Longarm chuckled. He lifted the
lamp's cowl, blew out the flame, and hung the lamp on
its post.

As he walked outside, Catherine stared at him over
the arm she still held over her mouth. In the moonlight
glistening in her hair spilling over her shoulders, he
could see that she was frowning curiously at him.

"Think I just found out what makes the wolves love
Crazy Kate so much."

"You don't think someone's been feeding them,
do you?"

"Not only someone but who."

Catherine opened her mouth to speak, but then

closed it suddenly. Several rifles barked in the west. Wolves snarled and yipped. Men shouted.

"Oh, no!" Catherine said, her voice quaking.

She and Longarm broke into a run across the farmyard.

Chapter 17

Longarm carried his rifle in one hand as he ran, pumping his arms and legs. He didn't worry about tripping.
The moonlight was nearly as bright as sunlight, delin-
eating all the rocks and shrubs and piles of discarded
lumber in his path.

Ahead, the desperate shooting continued. While the
men's shouts and cries dwindled, the yipping and snarling of enraged wolves grew louder. It all was emanating
from down a long hill strewn with boulders and spiked
with cedars and junipers. On Longarm's right, the black
ridge wall jutted against the stars whose light was
barely visible amid the incredible, buttery light of the
high-kiting moon.

He could hear Catherine running behind him though
he was gradually outdistancing her. Ahead, he could
see the flashes of the guns, the flames stabbing toward
his left, where wolf-shaped shadows flicked this way
and that.

Longarm stopped suddenly. Something moved downslope about twenty yards away. Two yellow eyes glowed. A man lay beside the wolf, writhing in pain. The wolf was shaking something in its teeth. An arm. Longarm could see two rings on the pale hand winking in the moonlight as the wolf shook the arm as though it were a rabbit.

Longarm raised the Winchester, planted a bead on the wolf's shoulder, nudged it up and back, and squeezed the trigger. The Winchester screeched loudly, flames stabbing from the barrel. The wolf lurched back and up, yipping before dropping the arm and piling up at its victim's quivering feet.

Longarm snapped a curse. Footsteps and heavy breathing grew louder behind him. He turned to see Catherine approaching. She'd lost her hat, and her hair blew in the wind, her eyes wide with alarm.

"Stay here," he told her, and then ran forward to drop beside the wolf. He placed a hand in the thick, knotted fur. The beast was still warm, but there was no heartbeat.

He went over to the wolf's victim. Catherine ran up beside him and crouched down over the bloody body.

"Sidney!" she gasped.

Ashton-Green, clothed in a fur coat but missing his hat, a thick scarf around his neck, moved his lips as he tried to speak, but then he gave a long sigh. He sagged back against the ground and lay still.

Catherine sobbed. The shooting and yelling and wolf snarling continued farther down the slope. Longarm leaped over Sidney and continued running toward where, while the guns roared, the shadows jostled around what appeared to be a pile of rocks.

A man screamed. A wolf howled victoriously and snarled especially loudly.

Another man shouted, and then there was only one rifle barking, stabbing flames at the silhouetted wolves surrounding the man.

So he wouldn't get hit by one of the bullets that the shooter seemed to be flinging every which way in his desperate attempt to keep himself out of the jaws of his attackers, Longarm dropped to one knee behind a boulder. Quickly, he slapped his Winchester butt plate to his shoulder and began picking out shadows and firing.

The echoes of the thundering reports hammered off the side of the ridge. Wolves yipped and squealed. The surviviors of Longarm's fussilade, confused and disoriented by the unexpected attack, retreated off down the slope.

Silence.

Longarm quickly thumbed fresh cartridges through the rifle's loading gate as he stared through the powder smoke that wafted like fog around his head, toward the nest of rocks ahead of him.

As he worked, he shouted, "Who's over there?"

The responding voice was weak, breathless. "Gen . . . General Fortescue. Is that you, Marshal Long?"

"Father!" Catherine yelled.

"Catherine! Good Christ—what are you doing out here?"

Longarm waved the girl to silence. "You torn up, General?"

"No. I was bit, but not bad."

"Then run this way while I cover you."

Catherine started to run to the general, but Longarm grabbed her arm and pulled her back behind the rocks. "Stay here. He'll make it."

"Father, hurry!" Catherine cried.

Longarm racked a fresh cartridge into the Winchester's breech then aimed in the general's direction, sliding the barrel left to right and back again, watching for wolves. The general's stocky, slightly stooped figure rose up out of the rocks where he'd sought refuge from the kill-crazy beasts, and began jogging up the grade toward Longarm and Catherine.

"Hurry, Father!" the girl called.

Aside from the howls of the wolf coming from the direction of the convent, which Longarm had become so accustomed to that he now only vaguely heard them, the night was silent. Nothing moved around the general. The man lumbered up the hill. When he was twenty feet from Longarm, the lawman walked out to grab the man's arm. Catherine ran to him then, too, and took the breathless, wheezing man's other arm.

"How bad are you hurt?" Catherine asked.

The man shook his head. "Just my leg. My hand. I'll be all right. We followed them down here from town, and they jumped us. Just like Indians, they surrounded and swarmed all over us."

"You think any of your boys are still alive down there?" Longarm asked, glancing over his shoulder.

"No," the general wheezed. "They were jumped immediately. I started firing and so did Sidney. That's how we got away. Sidney said he was going to try to get to town for help." He looked questioningly from Catherine to Longarm.

"He didn't make it, Father," Catherine said, grimly.

"It's okay. You're all right. We'll get you back to town. What a stupid thing to do in the first place!"

"Yes, yes, well—I've no defense except that I just didn't realize how many there are. How brave they are. I've never seen wolves like this."

As Longarm and Catherine continued guiding and steering the man up the hill, swinging wide around Sidney Ashton-Green's dark, bloody form, Longarm said, "I never have either. And for good reason. These wolves are being fed. Probably regularly and probably just enough to keep them wanting more. That's why there's so many of them, why they're so big and, likely, why they've become so brave!"

"*Fed?*" The General stopped suddenly and looked in shock at the tall lawman. "*Why? Who?*"

They'd just reached the top of the hill and were heading back in the direction of the farmyard when something flashed in the moonlight and inky shadows ahead. Longarm knew it was a gun before he heard the bullet screech about six inches off his left ear and spang off a rock behind him. A half second later, the rifle's thundering report vaulted around the canyon.

"Down!" he shouted, throwing the general behind a large boulder to his left and then quickly throwing Catherine down after her father. There were two more flashes in a low escarpment just ahead about thirty yards and to his right—a flash on each side of the scarp that appeared as a dark mound trimmed in silvery moonlight, bristling with moon-silvered and -shadowed junipers.

Longarm snapped his rifle to his shoulder and triggered one round where he'd seen each flash, then threw himself sideways behind the boulder. The bushwhackers cut down on him again, their slugs blowing up dust and gravel inches from his heels. He drew his legs behind the cover and pressed his back against the boulder.

Catherine put her hand on his shoulder. "Are you hit, Custis?"

"No. Not that they ain't tryin'!"

"Who's *they*?" asked the general, sitting on the other side of Catherine, with his back against the boulder, holding his bit hand in his lap gingerly. His gray hair and carefully trimmed mustache shone in the moonlight.

Longlarm pumped another shell into his Winchester's breech, gritting his teeth in fury. "Calvin and his big deputy." He doffed his hat and slid a cautious glance out around the boulder.

A gun on the low scarp's right side flashed. The bullet curled the air off Longarm's right cheek before plunking into the ground with a high, echoing whine behind him.

"Marshal Calvin?" Catherine said, shocked. "But *why*?"

"Ain't exactly sure, but I got a pretty good idea."

Longarm quickly snaked his rifle around the edge of the boulder and fired two quick shots. He waited until he saw a head-shaped shadow slide out from behind the scarp's right side, and he fired again. Because of the Winchester's momentarily blinding flash and the billowing gray powder smoke, he couldn't tell if he'd hit anything. But the bushwhacker's head was no longer where he'd last seen it.

He thumbed fresh shells through the long gun's loading gate, replacing the ones he'd spent. The general was breathing hard, raspily, on the other side of Catherine, who knelt beside Longarm, regarding him fearfully.

"What are we going to do?"

Before Longarm could respond, Calvin yelled from the other side of the escarpment, "Longarm, come on out of there. We know you got the girl with you. You come out, we'll let her live!"

"I know better than that, Calvin," Longarm returned, his voice echoing in the still, cold, quiet night. "You know we saw the barn. You'll want to make sure we both can't talk about it!"

"That's a promise, Longarm! You come out, the girl lives! I give you my word!"

"As an honest man?" Longarm laughed without mirth. "I tell you what—you and that giant come out, and I'll let you both live! You keep sending lead my way, you're gonna piss-burn me bad, and I'm gonna make sure neither one of you sees the next sunrise, let alone the next full moon!"

Silence.

Longarm turned to Catherine. "You stay with your father."

"What're you going to do?"

"I'm gonna circle around 'em. I want you to keep 'em entertained with this. But don't give 'em a target." Longarm extended the Winchester to her. "They'll think it's me. Just a shot every fifteen seconds or so oughta do it."

"You got it," she said with a resolute nod, pursing her lips. "You be careful. More than one breed of wolf out here, obviously."

"Yeah, obviously."

Longarm slid his pistol from its holster, spun the barrel across his forearm, rose, and glanced at Catherine. "All right."

As she snaked the Winchester around the side of the boulder, while keeping her head safely back behind the cover, and triggered a shot, Longarm ran straight back to the south. When he'd run fifty yards or so—far enough away that Calvin and Emil likely couldn't see him—he turned and followed a shallow, narrow gully west another fifty yards.

As he moved, he could hear Catherine firing his Winchester roughly every fifteen seconds. It kept Calvin and Emil busy, but he knew it was only a matter of time before the two crooked local lawmen tried circling around and flanking Catherine and her father. Occasionally, Calvin shouted something that Longarm couldn't hear above the shooting, but he assumed the town marshal was still trying to convince Longarm his situation was hopeless.

About twenty minutes after he'd left Catherine and the general, Longarm found himself nearly straight north of Calvin and Emil. He was a little higher, as well. Below, he could see the two men's rifles flashing every few seconds as they tried to get "Longarm" to deplete his own ammo and be forced to give himself up.

They hunkered behind the low, sandstone shelf, Emil to Longarm's far left now, Calvin to the shelf's right end.

Longarm moved out from behind a gnarled piñon and, crouching to make as small a target as possible, walked toward Calvin. The man must have spied his moon shadow. After firing another shot with his Winchester, the town marshal stiffened. He pumped a fresh cartridge into his carbine's breech and spun toward Longarm.

"Calvin, drop it!"

The man leveled the carbine. Longarm triggered the .44. Calvin triggered the carbine, but not before Longarm's bullet had punched a hole through the man's right side and knocked him backward. The local lawman's rifle belched groundward, blowing up a dogget of grass, gravel, and dust just off the tip of his right boot.

Longarm turned left as the giant spun with a startled grunt, bringing a rifle around. Longarm fired twice, one bullet crashing into a rock to the right and just behind Emil. The first bullet had found a home in Emil's left shoulder.

The giant cursed, dropped his rifle, then wheeled to his own right and ran off into a wash that trailed eastward from the shelf that he and his boss had been crouched behind.

"Hold it, Emil!" Longarm dropped to a knee to steady his aim, and fired twice quickly. Both bullets blew up dirt in the moonlight as Emil followed the wash into some giant rocks and cedars.

"Shit!" Longarm cupped a hand to his mouth, lifting his voice. "Catherine, hold your fire!"

Longarm bolted off his heels and ran forward, to where Calvin was sitting on his butt and reclining against the sandstone shelf, arms crossed on his belly, head sagging. He was breathing hard. Longarm tossed the man's carbine off into the rocks. He shucked Calvin's six-shooter from the holster under the man's heavy blanket coat and gave it the same treatment as the rifle.

"You bastard!" Calvin spat, looking up from beneath his hat brim, the hat tilted back and right. His face was pinched with fury. "Why the hell'd you have to come here? We had it made!"

"No time for hollow apologies, Calvin." Longarm ran out from the east end of the shelf and into the wash sheathed in high, mushroom-shaped rock formations stippled with cedars and sage shrubs. The moon had angled far to the west, leaving this narrow wash inky with darkness. Plenty of places for a man to hide in here. Longarm had to be careful.

He slowed his pace. The short hairs pricked under his coat collar. He had a feeling Emil was near, waiting.

Chapter 18

Longarm slowed his pace and tried to ease his breathing so he could listen for Emil.

He heard the rasp of a pair of heavy lungs, smelled a sharp sweat stench a half second before two big arms grabbed him from behind, pinning his arms against his sides. His breath left his lungs in a heavy *chuff* of expelled air as the dark ground slid away below and Emil lifted him one, two, three feet off the ground.

The giant grunted as he drew Longarm taut against him, literally trying to squeeze the life out of him. Longarm felt his head swelling from lack of oxygen as he kicked wildly, trying to free himself from the bearlike grip.

He rammed a boot heel against the giant's right knee. Emil grunted again, swung hard to his right, dipped, and drew his arms away suddenly, propelling Longarm to the ground at about sixty miles an hour. At least, that's how fast Longarm felt he'd been traveling when the ground slammed into the top of his head. It felt as though it had hammered his noggin six inches down into his torso.

His ears rang. His neck felt as though three railroad spikes had been hammered into it. Knowing he was in for a lot more, he tried to raise his pistol, but found that his hand was empty. He'd dropped the gun. Emil's huge shadow lunged toward him, the giant's anvil-sized boot connecting with Longarm's breastbone.

The lawman groaned, feeling as though his brisket were splintering around his heart, as he flew straight back against a boulder along the wash's bank behind him. He slumped to the wash's sandy floor, catbirds screaming in his ears. For a minute, sickness flooded him, and his guts convulsed. He thought he was going to throw up.

Knowing that Emil was likely about to pounce on him again made him suppress the urge. He lifted his head.

The giant was moving toward him. Moonlight limned the top of the barrel of the pistol in his hand. It also winked off the giant's big teeth as the man spread his lips in a devilish grin.

Emil's voice was so deep it seemed to be emanating from the bottom of a deep well. "End of the trail, lawman. Wolf bait. That's what you are."

A gun popped from upwash. Longarm saw the flash. Emil grunted as the bullet smashed into the side of his head. The giant teetered like a windmill in a cyclone, gave a groan and a long sigh, and then fell to Longarm's left with a heavy *thump*. Beneath the screeching in Longarm's ears came the crunching of boots. He glanced up to see a bulky silhouette growing larger as the person walked toward him. He could smell the odor of powder smoke mixing with the spicy fragrance of opium.

The figure stopped. Moonlight angling over the north wall of the wash shone on the side of Zeena Radulescu's face. It limned the brown hair blowing around the scarf wrapped over her head. The tassles of a cape rustled in the slight breeze, as did the hems of her dark wool skirts.

There was a click. Longarm sank back on his heels and watched a smoking pistol come up—the Remington .36 he'd emptied once earlier that evening. She aimed the gun at him. Her face in the milky moonlight looked as though it had been carved out of stone—that's how much expression it had.

Longarm said, "Don't tell me you still got your neck up over Kansas Pete." He paused while she stared at him, holding the gun steady in her black-gloved hand. "Or you just want Emil and me—and Calvin, of course—out of the way so you can have all that gold for yourself?"

"You knew?"

"I suspected Calvin and Emil . . . were up to somethin', just didn't know what. Now I know. And now I know you were in on it, too, helpin' keep the werewolf legend alive here in Crazy Kate."

"Who knows?" she said cooly. "It could be true."

"You don't believe that any more than I do. Oh, maybe some of the locals still do." Just then, right on cue, the wolf from the northern pinnacle of rock howled. "Obviously Crazy Kate herself still does. But she's likely genuinely crazy, thinks she really is a werewolf. You've just been usin' her like you been usin' the legend—to scare as many people out of town as you can, so you can have the gold for yourself—you, Calvin, and Emil, that was . . ."

"You're pretty smart for a lawman," Zeena said coolly. "Smarter than Calvin. He thought we could just stake a claim. Only you can't stake a claim on public property, of course. The marshal's office and jail belong to the town . . . as well as everything under it."

"So you cooked it all up." Longarm sighed, stared at the dark maw of the gun staring with cold indifference back at him. "You won't get away with it. Even with me dead."

"We'll see."

Zeena took one step forward, jutting the pistol at Longarm. There was another sharp pop. Only Zeena's gun didn't flash until a second after the pop. The flame stabbing from the .36's maw flew over Longarm's right shoulder, the bullet squealing off a rock high above his head.

The first pop had come from down the wash.

Zeena flew back in the direction she'd come, disappearing in the stygian darkness as she hit the floor of the wash with a thump. She groaned and struggled to rise—Longarm could hear the gravel crunching as she ground her heels into it. Then she gave a sigh and fell silent.

"Custis?" Catherine called. He could hear the girl running toward him. Now he saw her shadow jostling in the darkness.

"Look out!" Longarm said, his voice raspy from the pain shooting through his head, neck, and shoulders.

Too late, Catherine tripped over Emil, flew over the unmoving giant, and landed in front of Longarm, dropping the pistol with which she'd shot Zeena. She shook her head and climbed to her hands and knees, looking at what had taken her boots out from under her.

Turning to Longarm, she shook her head in wonder and said, "What's going on? I stopped back there a ways when I heard you and . . . him . . . fighting. But then she came . . . and I saw the pistol, heard your conversation . . ."

"Well, that about said it—a simple matter of greed," Longarm said, heaving himself to his feet and then pulling Catherine up, as well. "Where's the general?"

"I left him holding your rifle on Marshal Calvin, though I don't think the marshal's going anywhere or trying anything in his condition."

"Come on, then. Let's fetch 'em and get back to town before the wolves come back for another meal. I'll send someone out for Zeena and Emil tomorrow, if there's anything left of 'em by then." He gave a deep sigh. "Most likely, they'll be feedin' 'em one last time."

Later, when they'd made their way to town, Longarm half-dragging, half-carrying Calvin, with the man's left arm slung over the federal lawmen's shoulders, Longarm glanced at Catherine. "You best get your pa over to the doc's place—if he's there and not at Zeena's. I'll lock up Calvin in one of his own cells. The doc can tend him later."

Calvin grunted something under his breath that Longarm assumed was an unfavorable estimation of his, Longarm's, family history.

"I'll be all right," the general said. "I'm very curious to see this gold you're talking about, Marshal. The stuff you think motivated this entire dastardly charade."

They were mounting the porch fronting the

marshal's office, the general limping on his wolf-bit leg, Catherine beside him, her arm around him, Longarm and the half-conscious Calvin leading the way.

When Longarm had unceremoniously dumped the bloody town marshal onto the cot in the jailhouse's middle cell, he fished the keys to the Wolf Hold cells out of the man's coat pocket. At the same time, Catherine lit the lamp on the marshal's desk. Longarm walked out of the cell and over to the trapdoor leading to the Wolf Hold. He was mildly surprised to find the trapdoor open.

"Come on down if you can make it, General. I'll let Mrs. Jacobs and the boy out of their cell and show you what I'm talking about."

Longarm dropped into the hole. As the General and Catherine followed on the rickety wooden rungs, Longarm started down the corridor, and froze. The door to Goldie's cell was not only open, it lay on the floor in front of his cell, as though it had been blown out from inside. It was illuminated by a torch leaning out from a bracket in a paneled wall on the corridor's left side, on the other side of a small table.

"Who's there?" called Mrs. Leonard, her voice echoing around the cavern. The boy murmured and sobbed quietly.

"Marshal Long, Mrs. Leonard." Staring at the door in shock, Longarm turned to the door behind which the woman stood, staring through the small, barred window. "Gonna get you outta there."

He shoved the key in the lock, turned it, and opened the door. The woman stood there, looking terrified. The boy lay curled on the cot behind her, under the blankets, sobbing quietly.

"What . . . what happened?" Longarm said, turning away from the woman and continuing toward Goldie's cell. "Did you see, ma'am?" As he looked inside, none too surprised, given the condition of the door, to see that Goldie wasn't there, the woman stepped up behind him.

"He went crazy," the woman said in a high, thin voice, wringing her hands together. "And broke out and ran through the hole and that was the last I saw of him. He . . . it . . . was horrible. Oh, the noises he made!"

"You don't mean to say he . . . he turned into a werewolf—do you, Mrs. Leonard?" This from Catherine, who stood with her father near the ladder.

"*Yessss!*" the woman said, turning to face Catherine and her father, still wringing her hands. She had a blanket draped over her shoulders. "Oh, Lord—it is true, after all! I mean . . . I didn't see him. Only heard that awful, terrible roar. A wolf's roar! Why, Davy and I will remember it for the rest of our lives. Then he just dashed past our cell . . . and was gone!"

Longarm peered into the empty cell. He looked down at the door that had been ripped off its hinges. Likely the hinges had been weak to begin with. Old and rusty. Goldie just got fed up with being down here, wanted to get away, and managed to break the hinges and make a run for it.

Longarm placed his hands on the woman's shoulders. "You best take your boy and go home, ma'am," he said gently. "Rest assured, Goldie didn't turn into any werewolf. You've just had a terrible past few hours, and you're overwrought. You go on home and get some sleep. I'll fetch the doc for you."

The woman's voice was weak. "Yes, yes, I suppose you may be right, Marshal."

Mrs. Leonard moved into the cell, lifted her boy off the cot, and carried him over to the ladder. Longarm took the boy from the woman while she climbed, and then, when she'd reached the office above, he handed the child up to her through the hole. He turned to Catherine and the general, both staring at him skeptically.

Longarm chuckled. "Goldie ain't no werewolf. He just had an itch to be free after bein' incarcerated for three long years in the federal pen. Might even have a case of the rabies, poor bastard. But he's not a werewolf." He stepped past the pair, walking back down the corridor, past the smoking, flickering torch. "Come on. Let's see if my suspicions are right."

He stepped across the door to the end of the corridor. The wall at the hall's end was paneled in pine planks. As he'd seen before, between the cracks in the planks, something glittered brightly. Using his gloved hands, he ripped a plank from the wall frame, then another. He stepped back and set his hands on his hips, his breath catching in his throat.

"*Whoa!*" said the general.

"You can say that again, Father." Catherine stepped up beside Longarm in the narrow hall. "Is that really . . . *gold*?"

"I got me a feelin' it's not only gold but good quality gold, judgin' by the color." Longarm brushed a hand across the small chunks that shone in the wall. In some places, the wall was pitted, which meant that Calvin and Emil, possibly even Zeena, had pried some of the gold out.

"As you can see," Longarm said, "that beam up there has been replaced. That there is the old one. I got a feeling the earth shifted a little, and when it did, it exposed that big, fat, wide vein of gold. Calvin discovered it, and after his heart quit beatin' so fast and he'd hauled out some of the rubble, he decided to make full use of the werewolf legend to drive everyone he could out of town. The fewer folks here, the fewer he'd have to share the gold with.

"Or maybe he figured that with all the wolves he could lure in with dead deer an' such, he could drive everybody out. Hard to say. If he survives the night, we'll ask him. But that there is the werewolf legend, folks, and the reason there's so many big, hungry wolves in these parts."

They all stood staring at the gold chunks showing through the dirt in the earthen wall.

The general said, "When did you start to suspect . . . ?"

"When Calvin and Emil hauled the dead wolves off. They were gone a long time. I saw the gold showing between the planks when I threw Goldie into his cell, and then it hit me that they might be up to somethin'.

"I wasn't sure what that somethin' was, but now I realize they were off feedin' the wolves. I don't doubt they had a stash of dead deer somewhere outside of Crazy Kate. They wanted to take full advantage of the moon tonight, so they hauled some fresh meat over to the barn, to work the wolves into a frenzy. They followed Catherine an' me out from town. When they saw that we saw the barn, they knew they had to get rid of us fast."

Catherine shook her head in disgust. "He locked that poor, injured boy up down here just to help maintain the ruse. He knew he wasn't going to turn into a werewolf."

"That's about the size of it."

"What about the gold?" the general wanted to know, staring at it lustfully.

"Belongs to the town. Mrs. Leonard and everyone else around here is going to be rich right fast."

"Wait," Catherine said, turning to Longarm. "What about Zeena?"

"Calvin's woman. He brought her into it because he needed someone with the blood of the original settlers from the Old Country to help keep the others convinced that the legend was true. To help spook 'em, most likely, during every full moon."

And Kansas Pete was part of it, too, Longarm thought. Calvin had brought him into it because ole Pete was a damn good Curly Wolf and would be a good hand—not to mention a gun hand—when it came to mining the gold and getting it safely out of Crazy Kate. Zeena's story about her and Pete had most likely been hogwash. When Pete had failed to turn Longarm toe-down, Calvin had given her the assignment to get the federal badge toter out of their way before Longarm discovered their secret.

Longarm plucked the torch out of its bracket and drew a long sigh.

"It's been a long, terrible night," the general said, sober now. "I've lost many friends. I think I'll go to bed." He kissed his daughter on the cheek.

"We best get you over to the doctor, Father."

"In the morning, my dear. I'll be fine till morning. Unless I change into a werewolf," the old soldier chuckled as he climbed the ladder through the hole.

Catherine sighed and turned to Longarm. "What an awful thing Calvin has done. Will he be tried here?"

"Tried and convicted and hanged, most likely." Longarm placed his hand on the girl's back and ushered her toward the ladder. "I best fetch the doc for Calvin. Wouldn't want him to die and cheat the hangman. And then I could use a drink."

Upstairs, he closed the trapdoor and checked on Calvin, who slept restively, groaning and muttering. Longarm bit out a curse at the man and then followed Catherine back out into the cold night. He doused the torch in the dirt of the street.

"What about your prisoner?" Catherine said as a gust of wind blew her hair, making it shine like gold in the light of the westering moon.

"I'll hunt him down tomorrow. He won't be hard to track."

"Hope he's not a werewolf," Catherine said. From the way she stared up at him, brushing strands of hair from her face with her fingers, he couldn't tell if she was serious.

He chuckled as he walked away to fetch the doctor for Calvin and the Leonards.

Longarm was pumping away between Catherine's spread legs, when the wolf from the north ridge howled.

It was followed by another, similar howl from somewhere to the south.

Longarm stopped pumping. Catherine stopped moaning and writhing. She stared up at him, eyes startled. They both turned to the near window, through which weakening, pearl light angled.

The howling continued. Both wolves howled as though calling to each other, answering each other's plaintive, menacing wails.

Catherine opened her mouth to speak, but Longarm pressed two fingers to her rich, moist lips. "Don't even say it."

He continued making love to the girl.

But with slightly less vigor than before.

Watch for

LONGARM AND "KID" BODIE

the 413th novel in the exciting LONGARM
series from Jove

Coming in April!

GIANT-SIZED ADVENTURE FROM AVENGING ANGEL LONGARM.

BY TABOR EVANS

penguin.com/actionwesterns